It was a long ~~...~~
had been kis ~~...~~

So long that she had almost forgotten how it felt to have a large hand cupping the back of her head and warm lips exploring her face. She closed her eyes and relaxed into his embrace, her heart thudding against her ribs as his lips found hers.

When she opened her eyes he was looking intently at her, his dark eyes brilliant with desire.

"Let's go somewhere more comfortable and more private," he said huskily. He stood up, drawing her with him. "My room...or yours?"

Dear Reader,

This is the second story I have set in Valdecarrasca, an imaginary Spanish village inspired by about twenty real villages in the lovely part of rural Spain where I've lived for the past ten years. The first book in the series was *A Spanish Honeymoon* (#3789). Other characters in this book have appeared before. The story of Richard and Nicola Russell is told in *Turkish Delights*, published by Harlequin® in 1993, while Simón and Cassia Mondragon appeared in *A Night To Remember* (1996).

Nowadays many readers buy their books online and join in discussions about their favorite romances on message boards such as the one at **www.eHarlequin.com**.

As a World Wide Web enthusiast, I believe the Web can be used to enhance our enjoyment of reading. While writing this book, I made a list of Web sites with pictures and text related to the story and its background.

If you would like to have this list of URLs (Web site addresses), e-mail me at anne@anneweale.com. Please bear in mind that I do a lot of traveling and may be away when your e-mail arrives. I'll reply as soon as possible.

Happy reading!

Anne Weale

THE MAN
FROM MADRID
Anne Weale

HARLEQUIN®

TORONTO • NEW YORK • LONDON
AMSTERDAM • PARIS • SYDNEY • HAMBURG
STOCKHOLM • ATHENS • TOKYO • MILAN • MADRID
PRAGUE • WARSAW • BUDAPEST • AUCKLAND

ISBN 0-373-03793-7

THE MAN FROM MADRID

First North American Publication 2004.

Visit us at www.eHarlequin.com

Printed in U.S.A.

CHAPTER ONE

THE muffled jangling of a distant bell made Cally give a soft snarl, the way Mog did when something annoyed him. Though, by nature, both she and the large tabby cat were good-tempered beings from whom smiles and purrs were more characteristic. It was just that right now she was busy preparing the bedrooms for tonight's guests and didn't want to be interrupted.

Leaving the floor mop propped against the wall, she crossed the landing, catching a glimpse of herself as she passed a large mirror. Any resemblance between the figure in jeans, T-shirt, sneakers and household gloves and her real self, the high-flying young businesswoman, designer-suited and always immaculately groomed, was 'purely coincidental' as the disclaimers in books said, she thought with wry humour. Who, seeing her now, would guess that a week ago she had been chairing a meeting in London?

Running down the three flights of stone stairs that connected the floors in the tall old Spanish house, she hurried to open the left-hand section of the massive door. In times gone by, when it was fully open, it had allowed a mule and cart to pass through to the stable at the rear of the premises.

In the street outside the great door stood a man of the type Cally had sometimes imagined but never actually met: a Spaniard to die for.

Well over six feet tall and built in proportion to his height, he had hair as dense and glossy as a black labrador's coat and features that were a replica of those on the Moor's head fountain in the village. Unlike the Moor he didn't have a beard, only what might be designer stubble or merely the result of a mountain walker not bothering to shave for a couple of days 'on the hill' as the British walkers called their excursions into the mountains.

It was the heavy backpack he had shrugged off his broad shoulders and propped against his long legs that made her think he was a walker looking for a bed for the night.

He said, in Spanish, 'Good afternoon, *señorita*. I've reserved a room for three nights. My name is Nicolás Llorca.'

When someone, a woman, had made the reservation by telephone, Cally had assumed that Señor Llorca was a company representative, using the *casa rural* owned by her parents as an inexpensive base for his sales sorties in the area. During the week they rarely had Spanish guests and not many at weekends. Most of their visitors were foreigners like her father and mother.

'Please come in, *señor*. We weren't expecting you to arrive until later, but everything is ready for you,' she answered, in the fluent Spanish he was unlikely to guess was not her native tongue.

'Have you come far?' she asked, as he ducked his head to avoid hitting the lintel of the wicket door made in an era when Spanish country people were rarely if ever six-footers.

'Not far.' He left it at that. So far he had not smiled as men usually did when they met her—especially Spanish men.

Not the friendly type, thought Cally.

She said, 'I expect you'd like to dump your pack before you do anything else. I'll show you your room.'

Leading the way back to the top of the house, she wondered if the bed in the room she had planned to give him would be long enough for someone of his height. Perhaps it would be better to switch him to the room with a *cama de matrimonio* where he could lie diagonally.

The other double rooms had twin beds, but then most of the couples who came here looked as if, like her parents, they had given up sex some time ago. Cally had been told by a Spanish friend that, in rural Spain, the hurly-burly of the marriage bed came to an end at the menopause. After that husbands had to look elsewhere for those pleasures. If true, it seemed a sad state of affairs.

Opening the door of the room she had decided to give him, Cally walked in ahead of him.

'I hope you'll be comfortable here. There's a shower with plenty of hot water.' She indicated the door leading off the bedroom. 'Dinner is from half-past seven because we have a lot of foreign guests. We'd be grateful if you'd be at the table not later than nine. Our cook doesn't live in and likes to go home by ten. If there's anything you need, you have only to ask.'

While she was speaking, Señor Llorca had been giving the room a comprehensive glance, taking in the furniture that had seen better days before being refreshed and made harmonious by a coat of paint and some simple stencils, the inexpensive rush mats and the pictures picked up for a few hundred pesetas at *rastros*.

What he thought of it—whether it was better or worse than the rooms he was used to sleeping in—was impossible to tell.

'Thank you,' he said politely.

'There's a roof terrace with a nice view of the valley just across the landing. If you'd like a cold beer, there's an honour bar on the landing,' Cally informed him. 'It would be helpful if you'd bring used glasses down to the main bar when you've finished with them.'

With that she removed herself from his presence.

Left to himself, Nicolás opened his pack, took out his wash pack, put it on the end of the bed and started to strip off.

For reasons of his own, this morning he had left his car in the care of a reputable garage in a town ten kilometres away and spent the day following tracks through the mountains which eventually had led him here, to the village of Valdecarrasca, where he intended to stay for as long as was necessary to achieve his several objectives.

As the girl who had let him in had promised, there was an ample supply of hot water. Removing the fiddly little freebie of wrapped soap from the soap rack, he replaced it with his own larger bar, and enjoyed an all-over lather to remove the sweat brought on by a long tramp under a hot sun.

Although it was October, and the leaves on the vines he had passed on the road leading into the village were turning brown or dark red, the weather was still very hot by northern European and North American standards.

Thinking about the girl, as he used the freebie mini-bottle of shampoo on his hair, he was puzzled by her. All the people in these parts spoke two languages: Valenciano, the language of this region of Spain, and *castellano* or Castilian, the lingua franca of all Spain.

She had welcomed him in *castellano*, speaking it with an accent that would not have surprised him in his own milieu in Madrid but was unusual coming from a cleaner in a small village environment. But then her whole manner had surprised him: her self-possession, amounting almost to an air of authority, and her total lack of what he categorised as girly come-ons. He might have been sixty for all the personal interest she had shown in him.

Accustomed to a level of interest that might have flattered him when he was eighteen but that he could do without now, Nicolás found her indifference to him refreshing.

Thinking about her narrow waist and trim but rounded backside going ahead of him up the staircase, he found himself becoming aroused. Amusing oneself with country girls had been acceptable in his father's and grandfather's time. But it was not his style. There were plenty of sophisticated young women in Madrid willing to co-operate when he needed feminine companionship, and perhaps, one day, he would marry one of them. But unlike his brother he was under no obligation to choose a bride. Also having seen at close quarters the uncomfortable relationships into which marriage usually deteriorated after a few years, he was in no hurry to try it.

Turning the shower's control from hot to cold, he also switched his thoughts to the reasons he was here.

At six o'clock, Cally was laying the long table where everyone staying with them would eat, when she heard male footsteps on the stairs. Moments later she heard the Spaniard asking if anyone was about.

She went round the corner from the dining area of the ground floor into the lounge area. 'I'm here. How can I help you?'

He had shaved, she noticed, and changed into light-coloured chinos and a check cotton shirt in place of the jeans and navy T-shirt he had been wearing on arrival.

'I suppose it would be too much to hope that, in a building of this age, you have a socket where I can plug in the modem of my computer?' He was carrying a small black case.

When she was in Spain, a computer was Cally's lifeline. But she didn't tell him that. She said, 'The office has a modem socket. We're too rural to have broadband here, but we do have two telephone lines so you won't be blocking incoming calls. Just make a note of how long you're online, please.'

She showed him the small room, off the lounge, she had fixed up as an office. As it had no window, she switched on a wall light and desk lamp. The desk was clear of clutter. She gestured for him to use it.

'If your cable isn't long enough to reach the socket—'

pointing to where it was '—there's an extension lead you can use.'

'Thanks, but that won't be a problem. Do you have many guests who want to use the Internet?' He sounded surprised.

'Not many, but we do have business people staying here on week nights. Until you arrived with your backpack, I thought you were probably one of them. If you have any problems, just call. My name is Cally.'

When she would have left him, he forced her to pause by asking, 'What is Cally short for?'

'Calista...but no one uses it.'

'Would you rather they did?'

She shrugged. 'I've been used to the short form since childhood. Can I get you something to drink while you're picking up your mail?'

'A lager would be good.'

'Coming up.' She went to fetch it.

Like him, she had changed, he had noticed. Now she was wearing a black skirt that hugged her hips but was full at the hem and a T-shirt that showed the shape and size of her breasts, neither too small nor too heavy. Her waist was cinched by a red belt, and her shoulder-length hair, which earlier had been secured by one of those stretchy things, was now held by a red plastic clip. Like all Spanish women, she had pierced ears. He hadn't noticed her earrings earlier, but this evening she was wearing small silver beads that caught the light when she turned her head.

By the time she came back with a tall glass and a bottle of San Miguel on a small tray, Nicolás had logged on and was waiting for his emails to finish downloading.

He looked up at her and said, *'Gracias.'*

Without glancing at him or the bright screen, she murmured, *'De nada,'* and turned away.

She had a musical voice and good ankles, he noticed before she disappeared. Then, starting to open the emails, he forgot about her.

As Cally finished laying the table, her father came home. Shortly before Señor Llorca's arrival, he had gone to the *ferretería* in a neighbouring village to buy some screws. She knew why the errand had taken so long but, unlike her mother, she wouldn't make a sarcastic comment and he wouldn't make an excuse.

Cally had learnt long ago that her father and mother were not like ordinary parents. They were the adult equivalent of juvenile delinquents: irresponsible, bolshie, sometimes endearing, more often exasperating.

She had loved them when she was small but gradually, over the years, her affection had been eroded by the realisation that neither of them loved anyone but themselves.

Fortunately she had also had a grandmother—dead now—who had rescued her from some of her parents' worst excesses by paying for her to go to a boarding school in England and having her to stay for much of the holidays.

'Have all the punters shown up?' her father asked. When they were not in earshot, he always referred to his paying guests as the punters.

It had not been Douglas Haig's idea to take on a *casa rural.* As with most of their attempts to make money, or at least keep a roof over their heads, it was Cally's mother who had been the driving force. But he didn't mind running the bar and playing the genial host.

'Yes…all present and correct,' said Cally. 'I expect they'll be down before long.'

As she spoke, the wicket door opened and a small plump woman with an old-fashioned cotton wraparound pinafore over her dress came in. This was Juanita, a widowed neighbour who cooked the evening meal when Mary Haig had one of her migraines or, as now, was away.

Juanita and Cally were chatting in Valenciano when a couple who had introduced themselves as Jim and Betty came down the stairs. Their room had been booked by Jim whose surname was Smith. But it wouldn't have surprised Cally to learn that Betty had a different surname. That they might be in a partnership rather than a marriage mattered not a jot to her. She had never had a long-term partner or relationship herself. What other people did was their business. But Jim and Betty were of the generation who had grown up when 'living in sin' was something people frowned on, and it might be that they did not feel entirely comfortable about their present status. There has been an occasion when two elderly couples who hadn't met before had been staying at the *casa rural* and one of the women had made a remark about 'your husband' to the other, causing visible embarrassment. Since then, Cally had been careful never to jump to conclusions that might not be correct.

'Good evening. Would you like a drink? The bar is open,' she told them, as Juanita bustled away to start preparing the menu they had agreed on earlier.

Sometimes, when all the guests were reserved types, it was necessary to do some ice-breaking to encourage them to socialise. Tonight, however, they were all outgoing personalities and were soon talking nineteen to the dozen, the men discussing golf courses and the women comparing notes about children and grandchildren.

To her surprise, while pre-dinner drinks were still in progress, Señor Llorca appeared. This was unexpected. Even in country areas the Spanish had their evening meal much later than most of the foreigners, and in the big cities they dined very late indeed.

Her father had joined the golfing-talk group, and Cally was behind the bar, reading *El Mundo*, a Spanish paper she had bought that morning but hadn't had time to look at. As the Spaniard approached the bar, Juanita came to the hatch that connected the bar with the kitchen and asked a question.

Cally answered her, then turned back to face the Spaniard. 'Another San Miguel?' she asked.

'No, I'll have a glass of wine—red, please.' He sat down on one of the bar stools, which reduced his height slightly but still kept his eyes on a level well above hers.

'The house wine is "on the house", but if you'd prefer something better we have quite a good cellar.' She handed him their wine list.

As he scanned it, she studied his face, taking in the details that combined to give it as powerful an impact as the lean and authoritative features of the Moor who had once ruled this region and whose followers, by intermarrying with the indigenous people of Spain, had bequeathed their dark eyes and proud profiles through many generations to people living today.

In this man the evidence of his lineage was particularly striking. His cheekbones, the cut of his jaw, the blade-like bridge of his nose and, above all, his dark-olive skin and black eyebrows and hair, combined to give him the air of having stepped down from a painting of a time in Spanish history that had always strongly appealed to her.

He gave the list back to her. 'I'll try your house wine.'

Perhaps he couldn't afford the expensive wines, she thought, as she filled a glass for him. Though he didn't give the impression of being hard up. Lightweight, slimline computers, such as the one he had been using in the office, were usually a lot more expensive than bulkier laptops.

'You speak Valenciano,' he said, referring to her brief exchange with Juanita. 'Were you born in this village?'

Cally shook her head. 'I was born in Andalucia. I've lived in several parts of Spain. Which reminds me, I forgot to ask for your identity card when you arrived. We have to keep a record of our visitors. If you don't have it on you, later will do.'

'I have it.' He reached into his back pocket and produced a wallet. His identity card was slotted into one of the pockets designed for credit cards, of which he had an impressive array, she noticed.

'Thank you.' After making a note of the details, she handed it back, noticing, as he took it, the elegant length of his fingers and the absence of a wedding ring.

'Is there room at the table for me to eat with the rest of your visitors?' he asked.

'Certainly. We can seat twenty people. If we don't have a full house, the proprietor and I eat with the guests. But I ought to warn you that, although the others all live in Spain, they're unlikely to speak more than a few words of Spanish. They come from the expat communities on the coast where they don't need to be fluent, or even to speak Spanish at all.'

For the first time, he smiled at her. The effect of it startled Cally. Even when younger, she had never been as susceptible to masculine charm as most of her girlfriends. Now, at twenty-seven, she was almost immune to it. Yet when this man flashed his white teeth at her, she felt almost as powerful a reaction as if he had leaned across the bar and kissed her.

'I have some English,' he said. 'Enough to make polite conversation. But they'll be too busy talking to each other to pay much attention to me. If it's possible, I'd like to sit where I can talk to you...about this village and the valley,' he added. 'Or, if you will be busy keeping an eye on the guests, perhaps I can talk to the proprietor. Does he speak Spanish?'

'Not very much,' said Cally. 'Señora Haig has a better command, but she's away at the moment. I expect I can tell you whatever you want to know.'

'How long have you worked for them?'

Before she could explain that she didn't work for them, one of the guests came to the bar to have his glass refilled. 'Same again, please, love,' he said to Cally, and then, to the Spaniard, *'Buenas tardes, señor. Hace bueno hoy.'*

His Spanish accent was terrible, but his intentions were good, and the younger man smiled as he answered, in English, 'Good evening. Yes, it's been a very nice day and the forecast for tomorrow is the same. But then Spain's excellent weather is what brought you to this country, I expect.'

'You're right there, chum,' said the Englishman, visibly relieved that he wasn't going to have to stretch what was probably a very limited repertoire of Spanish phrases.

Cally was adjusting to the discovery that Nicolás Llorca spoke English with no trace of a Spanish accent. To speak it so perfectly, he must have learnt it very early in life and use it as frequently as she used his language.

She felt slightly annoyed that he hadn't made that clear to her. To tell her he had 'some English' had been deliberately misleading. Clearly, the man was bilingual and should have said so.

She wondered if he had minded being addressed as 'chum'. The Englishman hadn't intended to be offensive, in fact had been trying to be friendly. The trouble with the British was that they lacked an instinctive sensitivity to the manners and customs of other nationalities. Americans tended to be the same. They both assumed that the kind of easy familiarity they took for granted was acceptable everywhere. But sometimes it wasn't.

'No need to sit by yourself. Come and meet the rest of us,' said the Englishman, with a gesture at the other foreigners.

The Spaniard rose from his stool. 'Would you excuse me?' he said to Cally.

'Of course.' His courtesy pleased her. It would have annoyed her if he had just walked away, as if a general factotum in a *casa rural* was not entitled to be treated like a lady. It would have shown he was no gentleman.

She watched him being introduced, or rather introducing himself to the older people: shaking hands with the men, kissing the hands of the women with an easy gallantry that suggested he was at home in circles where the gesture was commonplace.

When Cally announced that dinner was ready if they would like to take their places at the table, the foreign guests formed pairs and chose seats side by side, leaving the chair at the head of the table to be taken by her father while she and Nicolás Llorca sat at the opposite end.

Again his sophisticated manners came into play when he drew out a chair for her before seating himself. None of the other men present had done it for their companions.

'Thank you, but why don't you sit next to Peggy? Then you'll have someone to talk to when I'm helping Juanita,' she suggested.

'Yes, come and sit beside me, dear,' said Peggy, patting the seat of the chair he had been holding for Cally and giving him a skittish look. She was old enough to be his mother but was refusing to surrender to late middle-age. Her hair was an unnaturally vivid auburn, her tan the result of hours of dedicated sun-bathing, her bosom a masterpiece of uplift.

For the first course there was a choice of fish soup or salad. Juanita ladled out the *sopa de pescado* for those who wanted it while Cally took round the plates of *ensalada* and small bowls of *alioli* sauce. Baskets of bread were already on the table, thick slices of the *pan integral* she preferred mixed with softer white bread, a concession to guests reared on steam-baked English factory bread whose teeth might not be equal to dealing with crusts.

Nicolás, as she was starting to think of him, was listening to some dramatic anecdote told by Peggy when Cally slipped into the chair on his other side. Casting an anxious eye in her father's direction, she recognised—though no one else would—signs that his neighbours' conversation was boring him. And when he was bored he reached for the carafe of wine more often than when he was interested.

She thought longingly of the day she was due to fly back to her real life in London. She didn't mind giving up two weeks of her holiday allowance to give her mother a break from Valdecarrasca, and her parents a break from each other. In some ways she enjoyed being here, surrounded by vineyards and mountains instead of city streets and traffic jams.

But being a commissioning editor for a major publishing house was no longer the secure, lifetime job it had been in the days when publishing had been famously described as 'an occupation for gentlemen.' Today it was a far more cutthroat business with take-overs and redundancies being as commonplace as in most other occupations.

What was worrying her at the moment was that Edmund & Burke, the imprint she worked for, had been taken over by a global corporation which had a new CEO. Everyone was waiting to see how this formidable woman, Harriet Stowe, would restructure the UK segment of the company. She had the reputation of being a ruthless decision-maker in whose view literary merit was unimportant compared with profitability. Edmund & Burke were famous for the quality of their books, but they didn't produce bestsellers. It was on the cards that Ms Stowe might decide to axe them.

This was not, therefore, a good time for Cally to be away from the office. But her mother's plan to visit a friend had been fixed long before the future of Edmund & Burke became uncertain, and Cally knew that, had the trip been postponed, her parents' marriage would also have reached a crisis point. She lived in dread of them deciding to separate for neither had the resources to survive on their own. They were not happy together, but apart they would be in deeper trouble, and the burden on Cally would be even heavier than it was already.

From the other side of the table, Fred, who was Peggy's companion, leaned towards Cally and said, 'I suppose the people in the village who own all the little vineyards are rubbing their hands at the thought of selling them off to property developers. They can see themselves getting rich, the way the Spanish who owned land on the coast did back in the sixties and seventies.'

'If the vineyards become building plots, the valley will lose all its charm,' said Cally. 'They'll make money, but they'll lose their quality of life. It's a pity there aren't more stringent planning laws. I don't think people should be allowed to spoil the mountains by putting up holiday villas wherever they want. There should be a limit above which nothing can be built.'

'There probably is,' Fred said, grinning. 'But the builders can get round that with a little of the old...' He demonstrated his meaning by rubbing his thumb against the tips of his fingers. Then, looking at Nicolás, he added, 'No offence meant, *señor*. But we all know it happens. Always has...always will.'

'My country is not the only place where graft is used to get round the regulations,' Nicolás answered dryly. 'Bribery exists everywhere. But I agree with Señorita Cally that it would be a pity if the uncontrolled development that has marred too many stretches of Spain's coasts were allowed to continue inland. On the other hand, people like yourselves—' with a gesture at the rest of the diners '—want to enjoy your retirement in a better climate, so some overdevelopment here is inevitable.'

Turning to Cally, he asked, 'What is your surname?'

'Haig.' She spelt it for him.

His black eyebrows shot up. 'You're half-British?'

'I'm all-British. That's my father at the end of the table.'

'So that's why you speak perfect English. I thought you were Spanish.'

'Your English is perfect too. How does that come about?'

'It's a long story. I'll explain some other time.' Although his answer came smoothly, she had an intuitive feeling that somehow her question had put him on the spot. She couldn't think of any reason why that should be the case, but she felt certain it was. For a moment she was tempted to press him, but she knew that it wouldn't be right when he was a guest, albeit a paying guest.

In any case it was time to clear the first course and serve the second. This was one of Juanita's specialities, *berenjenas mudéjar*.

'I know *berenjenas* are what the Americans call eggplants and we call aubergines,' Cally heard Peggy say to Nicolás, while she was taking the plates round. 'But what does *mudéjar* mean?'

As no one else was speaking at that moment, everyone heard his reply.

'*Mudéjar* refers to the Moors who stayed behind when Queen Isabella's army had forced the Arabs who ruled a great part of Spain into retreat. The Moslems who stayed became slaves, but they were valued for their artistic gifts. You see their influence in what's called the *mudéjar* architecture of the thirteenth century. This excellent dish is another reminder of how much this country owes to seven hundred years of Moorish culture.'

He lifted his glass of wine and looked at Juanita, still busy doling out steaming spoonfuls of baked sliced aubergines in a garlicky sauce. '*A la cocinera*...to the cook.'

As the others echoed his toast and Juanita beamed her gratification, Cally warmed to him on two counts: for his compliment to someone who was all too often ignored, and his grasp of his country's history.

She wished it had been her father who had answered Peggy's question and proposed the toast, but he never read books and he took the meals set before him, his clean clothes and all other creature comforts totally for granted. Perhaps it wasn't his fault. He had been spoilt by his mother, her other grandmother, and was not the only man of his generation who thought it a woman's duty to make things comfortable for the man in her life.

Which was one of the reasons why Cally had serious reservations about ever allowing another man into her life. She knew they were not all selfish encumbrances like her father, but many were, and it could be difficult to recognise a man's true nature when, in the early stages of a relationship, he was on his best behaviour.

'Hot plates. Now that is a treat,' said Peggy. 'So often, in Spanish restaurants, the plates are cold and it cools down the food before you've had time to enjoy it.' She gave Nicolás a friendly nudge with her elbow. 'I don't mean to sound critical 'cos I love Spain. I wouldn't go back to Birmingham if you paid me.' She lifted her glass and looked round at the others. '*Viva España!*'

Cally had just placed a plate in front of Fred. Across the table she caught Nicolás's eye. His face expressionless, he gave her a barely perceptible wink. It had a similar effect to his first smile: something turned over inside her.

Then, like the red light that flickered in the notification area of her computer's monitor screen when her virus protection program detected something nasty in an email attachment, a voice in her head said, Watch it! This guy is dangerously attractive.

The *berenjenas* were followed by lamb cutlets with brown earthenware bowls of the vegetables that the Spanish usually served separately but the British liked to accompany their meat course.

Finally, there was a choice of puddings: Juanita's home-made *flan*, Mrs Haig's home-made ice cream, or Cally's fruit salad, laced with kirsch.

'You give excellent value for money,' said Nicolás, who had waited for her to sit down before starting to eat his *flan*.

'We try to. It's the way to bring people back. But we have strong competition from other *casas rurales* in the region. What made you choose this one and how did you find us?'

'I read a book by Rafael Cebrián about the mountains in this area. He describes a place called the Barranc de L'Infern, which sounds an interesting challenge. Have you heard of it?'

Cally nodded. The name meant the ravine of hell and everything she had heard made it sound a place to avoid. 'There've been several accidents there...some of them fatal. It's particularly dangerous after rain. You shouldn't attempt it alone. You might never get out.'

'Don't worry. I'm going to go through with some guys who know what they're doing.' He paused, looking into her eyes with a curiously intent expression. 'But I'm glad you're concerned for my safety. When I arrived here, I had the feeling you didn't much like the look of me.'

This was so far from her first reaction on seeing him—that he was the most fanciable male she had seen in a long time—that she almost laughed.

Instead she said coolly, 'I'm sorry if I seemed unwelcoming. I didn't mean to. Excuse me, I need to attend to the coffee.'

In the kitchen, Juanita said, 'How long is he staying, the Madrileño?'

'Three nights. How do you know he's from Madrid?'

'His voice…his manners…his air. He's very handsome, don't you think?'

'Paco is handsome,' said Cally, referring to the best-looking young man in the village who was a worry to his mother and had broken several girls' hearts.

'*Paco es uno desgraciado,*' said Juanita contemptuously. 'You can't compare that good for nothing with a man of education and breeding. I worked for the upper classes when I was young. I recognise a gentleman when I see one.'

'You're a snob,' Cally told her, smiling. 'There are as many bad lots among the rich and the aristocrats as among ordinary people. Probably more.'

'That's true,' the cook conceded. 'They're no better…but also no worse. Wouldn't you rather be a rich man's pampered wife than a poor man's slave like your mother?'

She was devoted to Mary Haig but, having herself had a husband who spent too much time in bars, took a disapproving view of Douglas.

'I would rather stand on my own feet and be independent,' said Cally.

'You can say that now, while you're still at your best. You won't always be young and attractive. A time will come when you'll want some babies and a man to keep you warm in bed. I know you have a fine career in London, but when you are thirty-five you may not find it so satisfying.'

At the dining table, Nicolás was listening to Peggy but thinking about Cally. He had perfected the art of seeming to be engrossed by older women's conversation while following his own train of thought at his mother's dinner parties. Sometimes she roped him in to fill a gap and, though such occasions bored him, he felt an obligation to help her out when he could.

His mother was very rich, and had once been a beauty, but now she was deeply unhappy because cosmetic surgery could not preserve the ravishing face she had had in her youth and none of her husbands and lovers had lived up to her expectations. So now she was a pill junkie, filling her days with meaningless social engagements and pouring out her troubles to several shrinks and any of her five children who could be persuaded to listen to a tale of woe heard many times before.

Seeing at a glance that Cally's father was what his American friends called a lush, Nicolás wondered why a girl of her obvious intelligence was wasting herself as a maid of all work in the backwoods of rural Spain. With her ear for languages, there must be better things for her to do.

He saw her coming back with the coffee tray and sprang up to take it from her.

'Oh…thank you.' When their fingers touched as she surrendered the tray to him, a charming flush gave her cheeks an apricot glow.

She wasn't tanned like the other women. Her complexion suggested she spent little time in the sun. He preferred her creamy pallor to the almost orange colour of Peggy's skin. Cally was like a solitary lily in a bed of garish African marigolds, he thought. Not that he disliked his fellow guests. He admired their courage in uprooting and transplanting themselves. They were enjoying their lives, more than could be said for his mother in her *palacio* in Madrid, or indeed for most of his bored and world-weary relations.

When Cally went to bed, most of the guests had already gone to their rooms. But her father, the man called Bob and Nicolás were still talking and drinking in the lounge. Nicolás was not drinking as much as the other two. In fact he had had only two or three glasses the whole evening. He wasn't talking as much either, just asking the occasional question and listening intently to their replies.

She hoped he would go to his room soon, before it became obvious her father had drunk too much.

In bed, she turned with relief to the book she was reading, an out-of-print history of the early days of air travel that she found far more absorbing than the current crop of short-lived bestsellers. When the church clock struck eleven for the first time, she put it aside and turned out her bedside lamp. By the time, a few minutes later, it repeated the eleven chimes, she was settled down ready to sleep.

But when it began to strike midnight she was still awake, her mind in a whirl of uncertainty about the future. At half-past midnight she got up, shrugged on a thin cotton robe and took her small torch from the bedside table.

There were no sounds from below as she padded barefoot down the stairs, the tiled treads cool under her soles. The ground floor was in darkness. Someone, probably not her father, had remembered to switch out the lights.

In the office, she booted up the desktop computer she used while she was here and logged on to the Internet, hoping there might be an email from Nicola.

Nicola and her husband were both publishers. Richard Russell was the head of a big firm, Barking & Dollis, and Nicola was co-director of Trio, a much smaller firm. Having been through the misery of redundancy herself—in fact she had been sacked by the man who was now her adoring husband—Nicola was sympathetic to Cally's anxieties and had promised to let her know if she heard any book trade gossip concerning Cally's new boss.

Disappointed when no emails downloaded, Cally went to a favourite website that supplied links to the world of arts and letters. But there was nothing new there and, frustrated, she shut down the machine and went to the kitchen for a glass of water.

Three clean wine glasses were standing upside down on one of the worktops. Had Bob washed and dried them? She doubted it. His wife had said during dinner that he was useless in the kitchen.

That meant that the Madrileño, as Juanita called him, must have dealt with them. Which also meant that he had stayed in the lounge until her father finally called it a day. Cringing at the thought of Nicolás seeing her father in his cups, and perhaps even assisting his unsteady progress up the staircase, Cally put the glasses away.

Everything he had said and done had supported Juanita's conviction that he was a *caballero*, the Spanish word that meant literally a horseman, but also the possessor of all the chivalrous qualities that distinguished a gentleman from lesser men.

Cally drank a tumbler of spring water brought from a *font* in the hills and made her way back up the stairs. Reluctant to return to bed, she decided to spend half an hour sitting outside on the roof terrace. As, unlike most Spanish houses, the *casa rural* had no *patio*, the terrace was the only place to enjoy some fresh air.

Except during cold snaps, the glazed door to the terrace was always left open, with a curtain of metal strands preventing flies from getting in. As she drew the curtain aside, she saw that one of the guests had had the same idea.

The cane armchair she had intended to sit in was occupied by Nicolás. His legs were crossed at the ankles and his bare feet were propped on the seat of another chair. Comfortably curled on his long lap was her parents' cat, Mog, who normally made himself scarce when there were strangers in the house.

CHAPTER TWO

IF HE had been lost in thought, he reacted fast to the metallic rustle of the fly curtain as she swept it to one side. But he didn't make a startled movement as she would have done.

Nicolás glanced over his shoulder, saw her standing in the doorway, and scooped the cat off his thighs before standing up and saying, in a quiet voice, 'It's too fine a night for sleeping. Come and join us. I've been making friends with your cat. I assume he's the house cat. Or is he a neighbourhood cat who uses your terrace?'

'He's ours,' said Cally, stepping on the terrace. 'My mother was walking the dog she had a few years ago. They were crossing a dry river bed when she heard a kitten mewing. It was inside a plastic bag with the rest of the litter. They were about a week old. All the others were dead.'

Her tone was dispassionate, but even now, years later, remembering the incident made her blood boil with disgust for whoever had been too mean and heartless to dispose of the unwanted kittens humanely.

Nicolás's response was equally unemotional. 'There are some rotten people in the world,' he said.

He was holding the cat as if it were a baby, on its back with his forearm under its spine and his other hand tickling its tummy. Mog, who normally disliked being touched by strangers, wasn't lashing his tail but purring deep satisfied purrs.

Unbidden and unwelcome, the thought came to Cally that being held and caressed by Nicolás might cause her to purr as well. She rejected the notion as soon as it entered her

26

mind. It must be the time of the month when her hormones were on the rampage.

The man was a stranger. She knew next to nothing about him. Because he had a way with cats didn't mean he was equally good at making love to women. Even if he were, she was not into casual sex. She was not into sex, period. It was a snare and a delusion devised by Nature to trick people into perpetuating the species, though the trick didn't work as well now that women had control of their bodies, at least to the extent of not getting pregnant. Controlling their reactions to the opposite sex was harder. But she had seen too many colleagues having their lives made wretched by disastrous relationships to want to risk it herself.

'It's very quiet here at night,' said Nicolás, moving to sit on the low flat-topped wall that surrounded the terrace but in places was ranged with plant pots.

'Some of our guests find the church clock disturbing.'

Against her better judgment, but reluctant to return to her room when the surrounding mountains were bathed in moonlight and the October night air was as balmy as a fine summer night in the UK, Cally sat down in the armchair he had vacated. Although she had a white lawn nightdress under her ankle-length robe, she was conscious of being without a bra or briefs. Perhaps this was because, apart from having bare feet, Nicolás was still dressed.

'On the way to bed, I was looking at the bookshelves on the next landing. Would it be all right if I borrowed one to read in my room?'

'Of course…that's what they're there for. But not many of our guests are bookworms. Mostly they're TV-watchers.'

'Did your parents build up the library, or did they inherit it from the previous owners of the house? Your father mentioned that he and your mother only set up the business about six years ago and had a bit of a struggle to get it going.'

'It wasn't easy at first. Some of the Spanish and all the German books came with the house. The last owner was a German botanist. A lot of the books I've found on *rastros* or in the secondhand paperback libraries catering to foreigners. The prices are low because most people take them back for a half-price refund, but I usually keep them.'

'You would enjoy the bookshops and book fairs in Madrid. Have you been to my home town?'

'Once, when we were living in the south, we had to get to England in a hurry for a family funeral. We put the car on the train at Algeciras and got off in Paris, with a stop of some hours in Madrid en route. I wanted to see the Goya paintings in the Prado, but it was closed that day. Juanita, who is cooking for us because my mother is away, went to Madrid last spring on a coach with other *pensionistas* from the village. She had a wonderful time. Have you always lived there?'

'No, I was born and grew up in the country. I enjoy Madrid, but—' He broke off as the cat suddenly sprang from his arms to the ground and then jumped onto another part of the wall and peered over the outer edge of it.

'He's heard something moving about under our neighbour's roof tiles,' said Cally, as Mog vanished. 'He fancies himself as an ace hunter, but I've never known him to catch anything. You were saying you enjoy Madrid, but...'

'But I wouldn't want to live in a city all the time. It's exciting and stimulating, but it can get a bit frenetic. I like to escape now and then.'

Cally was struck yet again by the fluency of his English but hesitated to press him for the explanation he had promised 'some other time.'

'Your situation is the reverse of mine,' he went on. 'Don't you ever feel bored with Valdecarrasca? Does it offer enough excitement and stimulus for you?'

She debated telling him that she didn't live here on a

permanent basis and in fact was only an occasional visitor. But she didn't feel inclined to talk about herself while there seemed to be things about himself he preferred not to divulge.

She said, 'Nowhere is dull or isolated now that we have all resources of the World Wide Web at our fingertips.'

'Do you spend a lot of time on the Web?'

'Quite a lot. How about you?'

'I subscribe to a couple of forums and read certain online columnists. What sort of things do you do?'

Cally had the feeling they were fencing with each other, neither wishing to reveal themselves. Yet all the time she was conscious of how attractive he was. She liked the way his hair sprang from his broad high forehead, the clear definition of his chin, the way the moonlight accentuated the slant of his cheekbones under the taut dark skin.

In her late teens, when she had sometimes indulged in romantic daydreams, this was the kind of face she had visualised but never seen in real life. Her parents had been living in Tarragona province then, and the Catalan men in that area had not been remarkable for their looks.

'Mostly I read the book reviews at online bookshops. Sometimes I look at what's on offer at the auction houses. The great thing about the Web is that it's all things to all men...and all women,' she said, smiling. 'Whatever you're interested in, you can find stuff about it and people who share your enthusiasms.'

'Some people even find partners, one hears.'

Cally shrugged. 'So they say. Perhaps, if one's looking for a partner, it's a good place to find one. I've often thought that people who aren't good-looking are at a huge disadvantage in the real world. They may have wonderful minds but they get written off because their faces aren't pretty or handsome.'

The church clock struck a single note. It was one o'clock

in the morning, she realised, and in five hours' time her alarm clock would wake her so that she could have an hour on the Internet before it was time to shower and dress and fetch *barras* of freshly baked bread for the guests' breakfast.

'Would you like a packed lunch tomorrow?' she asked.

'Is that part of the service?'

'When we have mountain walkers staying with us—yes. We charge for the ingredients but not for the preparation. If you have a flask, we'll fill it with coffee or tea. What would you like in your bread? *Jamón serrano*…cold chicken… sheep's cheese and lettuce…*chorizo*?'

'*Jamón serrano* would be excellent. I'd like to leave about nine, if that's convenient? What time is breakfast?'

Cally stood up. 'Most people have it between eight and nine. But you can have it as soon as I get back from the baker's at half-past seven, if you like.'

'Let's say quarter to eight.'

'Okay…goodnight.'

As she moved towards the doorway, he stepped ahead of her and swept the curtain aside.

'Thank you.' She had to pass very close to him to go through the opening. As she did so, she found herself wondering what she would do if he put his hand on her waist and turned her to face him.

But he only said, '*Buenas noches.*'

As the curtain fell into place behind her, Nicolás wondered what she would have done if he had obeyed his impulse to kiss her goodnight.

All the time they had been talking, he had been conscious that under her modest dressing gown and long filmy nightgown she had been naked. For some reason, although there was nothing overtly sexy about her, in her presence he was always aware of how soft she would feel under his hands.

While he had been stroking the cat, a part of his mind had been thinking about stroking Cally.

Looking over the wall, he saw that the cat had its nose close to the edge of a Roman tile and was quivering with frustration because it couldn't reach whatever was lurking under the tile.

I know the feeling, *amigo*, thought Nicolás. Leaving the cat to its fruitless vigil, he left the terrace and, switching on the landing light, selected a couple of books he had noticed earlier to distract him from thinking about Douglas Haig's tempting daughter.

When, next morning, Cally went downstairs, the first thing she did was to fill the kettle with *font* water that had also been filtered to remove some of the *cal* that quickly furred up the kettle. Her mother was always complaining about the hardness of the local water and the damage it did to her skin.

A little later she was walking back from the village bakery when to her surprise Nicolás came out of a sidestreet leading towards the vineyards. He was wearing a yellow singlet and black shorts and had obviously been for a run. He wasn't out of breath but his skin was glistening with sweat and his black hair was damp, showing a tendency to curl at the nape of his neck.

'How far have you run?' she asked, as he fell into step beside her.

'About five or six kilometres. The lanes through the vineyards are perfect...hardly any traffic.'

'I know. I use them for walking. Do you run every day?'

'Most days.' He used his forearm to wipe some trickles from his forehead.

He was not, she noticed, as hairy as many Spaniards. Some women liked hairy men but her preference was for a smooth chest and only a light dusting of hairs on a man's arms and legs. Enough to be unmistakably masculine but not reminiscent of a gorilla.

She caught herself thinking that Nicolás had exactly the right amount of body hair, at least as far as she could see. The thought was followed by another: what the hell am I doing appraising his body like this?

She was not the only one. A couple of young village women, on their way to the bakery, eyed him with interest as they exchanged good mornings with Cally. Knowing how their minds worked, she guessed that they would be wondering if he was one of the *casa rural*'s visitors, or someone she had in tow.

At the house, he pushed open the door for her, but did not follow her in. 'I need to do some cool-down exercises. I won't be long.'

Carrying the bread to the kitchen, Cally wondered if the woman across the street who kept a close eye on the comings and goings from their house was getting an eyeful of the tall stranger stretching various areas of his muscular anatomy. He must be in great physical shape to be able to run that distance and get back looking as if he could do it again if necessary. Occasionally she met holiday-makers jogging among the vineyards and looking fit to collapse.

The next time she saw him he had showered and changed into clean clothes. He had brought down a flask to be filled.

'The notice on the back of the bedroom door says you have laundry facilities? What does that mean?' he asked.

'If you leave whatever you want washed in the big plastic bag that you'll find in the wardrobe, it'll be collected when your room is done and ready to wear by tonight.'

'That's better than five-star hotels. They often take twenty-four hours to turn around personal laundry.'

'We aim to please,' said Cally, smiling. 'Would you like a cooked breakfast? I can do you a French omelette, or bacon with a fried egg and mushrooms, or a piece of grilled haddock with tomatoes.'

'Is an omelette with tomatoes and mushrooms possible?'

'Certainly. But I won't cook it till you've finished your selection from the breakfast buffet. You'll find it round the corner. I take it you'd like coffee to drink?'

'Yes, but *descafeinado* rather than the real stuff, please.'

He didn't drink much. He didn't kick-start his day with strong shots of caffeine like many of the people she knew in London. What were his vices? she wondered. Most people had some.

When she brought him a cup of coffee, he had already drunk a tumbler of orange juice from the jug on the buffet and was eating a bowl of muesli.

'Is it today you're doing the Barranc de L'Infern?' she asked.

'Tomorrow. Will the people I met last night still be here this evening?'

She nodded. 'I'll start your omelette.'

When she brought it to him, he said, 'Don't go away. Stay and talk to me. Apart from surfing the Web, how else do you amuse yourself?'

'There's no shortage of things to do. There are cinemas not far away, and art exhibitions and reading groups. Also, once you get on the *autopista*, it's not much more than an hour to Alicante and Valencia, both of them very lively cities.'

'I know. I've been to them. Do you go there often?'

'Fairly often.'

This was true. When flying to and from Spain, as she did several times a year, she used both cities' airports. She liked Valencia's airport best. It was quieter, used mainly by Spanish business people rather than the package holiday tourists who poured into Alicante, the gateway to such popular resorts as Benidorm and Torrevieja.

'You haven't explained how you found us,' she reminded him.

'On the Web. I was looking for sites about the rock-climbs in this area and found a site belonging to two professional climbers. There was a link to another site with a list of all the *casas rurales*. Yours seemed the most convenient for the things I wanted to do. Do you get many enquiries via your webpage?'

'Not at first, but now more and more people are using the Web for looking for and booking holidays. I picked up an email from a prospective visitor this morning. He wanted to know if we do vegetarian meals.' Remembering that Nicolás's reservation had been made by telephone, she said, 'You had someone telephone us rather than booking by email. Why was that?'

He shrugged. 'I'm not sure. Perhaps the person I asked to make the booking was more comfortable with the telephone than email. If I wanted to extend my time here, could I do that?'

'Certainly.' It annoyed her that the prospect of him staying longer pleased her on a personal level as well as from a business point of view.

'I'll let you know tonight. How will you spend your day?'

'This morning I'll work. This afternoon I might drive to the coast and swim. The sea will still be warm but the beaches won't be as crowded as they are in the summer.'

'Yesterday, when I arrived, you were doing housework. Do you do that routinely, or is your parents' regular cleaner off sick?'

The frank answer was that her mother had a problem keeping household help. She tended to lose her temper when things weren't done her way. At the time Cally was born, so she had been told, it had been possible for retired ex-colonials, settling in Spain, to employ several staff and pay them low wages. But those days were long gone. Young

Spanish women had jobs in offices, shops and supermarkets, and even for their mothers and grandmothers there were now alternatives to domestic service. Those who still did cleaning expected to be treated as equals and Mrs Haig's haughty manners had not endeared her to the helpers who had come and gone, usually after a stormy altercation.

But Cally was not about to reveal this to Nicolás. She said, 'Not many women want to do other people's housework as well as their own nowadays. It's understandable. Actually I find it rather satisfying.' Though I wouldn't want to do it full-time, was her unspoken addendum.

He gave her another of those disconcertingly intent looks. 'It seems a waste of your capabilities.'

'You don't know that I have any other capabilities,' she said lightly.

'You read. You're a linguist. Your whole appearance and manner indicates intelligence and initiative. You have the computer skills that are essential in most jobs today. I'd say you could handle any number of interesting careers.'

It was on the tip of her tongue to tell him she had a career that delighted and fulfilled her, but somehow to say that seemed to be tempting fate to snatch it away from her.

'Thank you for your confidence,' she said, with more warmth than she had shown him so far. 'Normally I don't pry into guests' backgrounds unless they volunteer information. But I have to admit I'm curious about what your work is.'

He smiled and it had the same effect as before. Something inside her melted.

'Have a guess?' he suggested.

She could visualise him in a doctor's white coat, or an airline captain's uniform or even, because he had so much charisma, as a TV presenter on one of the more intelligent programmes. But if he were the latter, Juanita would have recognised him from the pages of *Hola!* the popular Spanish magazine that had spawned *Hello!*.

'Something scientific perhaps?'

He shook his head but, before he could tell her what he did, they were joined by Peggy and Fred.

To Cally's annoyance, after Peggy had said good morning, she added archly, 'Are we interrupting something. Are we *de trop*, as the French say?'

Nicolás had risen to his feet. He said pleasantly, 'Not at all. I'm just off. That was an excellent omelette, Cally. Thank you. I'll be back in good time for dinner.'

Disappointed that she hadn't found out what he did, Cally said, 'You'll find your packed lunch and your flask on the worktop just inside the kitchen door.' She turned to the others. 'Would you like something cooked for breakfast?'

After all the guests had gone out for the day, and her father had gone to play golf with his two particular cronies, Cally heaved a sigh of relief at having the house to herself for a few hours. She left Nicolás's room till the last. As she made beds, changed towels, mopped floors and emptied the contents of waste paper baskets into a black bin bag, she thought about Nicolás's occupation and found herself wishing she were with him, climbing some steep mule track surviving from the days when most journeys were made on foot and the quickest route between many villages was by way of trails laid by the Moors long ago.

When she unlocked the door of his room, she felt a bit like Bluebeard's wife entering the forbidden chamber. Which was a silly feeling to have. He was just another guest, a transient visitor she would most likely never set eyes on again.

He had left the plastic laundry bag on the upright chair near the door. It contained the T-shirt and jeans he had worn on the day he arrived, the sports shirt he had worn last night and his running kit. But no undershorts or socks. Their absence was explained when she went into the shower room and found them hanging on the shower rail, already almost dry. He must have washed them the night before.

He had also made the bed and, instead of the clutter of possessions left lying about in the other guests' rooms, tidied away most of his belongings. On the bedside table were two books borrowed from the shelves on the landing, the top one being *The Wandering Scholars*, a classic, written in the twenties, about life in mediaeval Europe. The one underneath was a travel book she would have liked to publish had the typescript been offered to her instead of to a commissioning editor with another publisher.

Cally took his laundry downstairs to load it into the washing machine. Then, in an involuntary act that troubled her all afternoon when she used her mother's car to drive to the coast, she lifted his bundled-up shirt and buried her nose in its folds. She knew that even scrupulously clean people left traces of their natural scent on their clothing, but he hadn't worn the shirt for long enough to do that. But his running singlet did carry his scent and, far from being unpleasant, it conjured up a vivid memory of his athletic body and its polished bronze sheen. She found herself trembling slightly, swept by feelings long repressed and believed to be under control. But, suddenly, they were not, and she was afraid of where they might lead her.

At first, when he mentioned extending his visit, she had been pleased. But now she thought that the sooner he went the better for her peace of mind. She had enough on her plate, professionally, at the moment without getting out of her depth on a personal level.

Nicolás ate his lunch sitting in the sun in the garden of a long-deserted house.

As well as the long brown *barra* filled with Spanish

mountain ham and cut into three sections, Cally had provided him with a banana, an apple and some green-skinned but sweet tangerines. For dessert there was a bar of plain black chocolate and a substantial chunk of *pan de higo* which was made from dried figs embedded with almonds.

Thinking about their conversation earlier, he had the feeling that Cally was in a no-win situation that was fine for her parents but a disaster for her. In his own family, some members made use of other members, though never of him. He had learnt early on to make his own decisions and stick to them.

A possible reason for her failure to assert herself and get a life of her own was the fact that she had grown up in a country of which she was not a national. In practical terms, she wasn't British but nor, despite her fluency with the language, was she Spanish. He had noticed that the children of diplomats often felt a sense of displacement. They lacked the deep roots of people raised in the country where they were born.

He had spent a lot of his own life outside Spain because his father's profession had taken him overseas and, after his parents' divorce, Nicolás had spent more time with his father than with his capricious, self-centred mother. But despite this cosmopolitan background, at heart he felt wholly Spanish. This land was where he belonged. Where did Cally feel she belonged? Probably nowhere.

Remembering her remark that, on the *autopista*, it wasn't much more than an hour's drive to Valencia or Alicante, he thought of the fast car he had left in a garage because it would attract too much attention in the village car park.

Maybe, if he extended his time here, he could take her out for an evening of sophisticated pleasures. Unless there was a boyfriend in the background.

It was hard to believe that an attractive *chica* of what—

twenty-four? twenty-five?—would not have a man in her life, but his feeling was that she didn't.

By the time he had finished eating, it was the hottest part of the afternoon. As a child he had seen the workers on his maternal grandfather's estates lying down in the shade for a *siesta*. Having read *The Wandering Scholars* until the church clock struck three this morning, he decided to take a nap under the drooping branches of an old fig tree.

When he woke up it was cooler. He went back inside the house and prowled its large empty rooms, considering various possibilities for its future.

When the guests assembled for pre-dinner drinks that evening, they all had tales of their days' activities to tell.

Fred and Peggy had had lunch at another *casa rural* an hour's drive away. 'But we didn't like it as much as yours,' Peggy told Douglas Haig. 'It was modern. It had no atmosphere.'

Tonight she was wearing a clinging red dress and dangling diamanté earrings which Cally felt were over the top for the setting which was rustic rather than glitzy. She suspected that Peggy was hoping to make an impression on Nicolás, which seemed ridiculous in the light of their respective ages. But perhaps Fred didn't give her the attention she craved. He seemed the down-to-earth type. Cally would have expected Peggy to be married to someone more dashing: the kind of man who, when going out in the evening, wore a blazer with a foulard cravat inside the collar of his shirt and had a moustache or a carefully trimmed beard.

When Nicolás appeared and came to the bar, he was wearing the shirt she had washed and ironed for him.

'Did you press my shirt?' he asked.

'Yes.'

'Thank you.'

She used the phrase often heard in Spain when someone

was responding to thanks. '*De nada.* It's part of the service. What would you like to drink?'

'A glass of the house red, please.'

As she filled a glass for him, she asked, 'Did you have a good day? Where did you go?' She assumed he had a map of the area and would know where his route had taken him.

'An excellent day…and I enjoyed my lunch. It's years since I had any *pan de higo*.'

'It's one of my weaknesses. I like fresh figs best, when they're available, and dried figs are good too, but the local dried figs are small and at this time of year the figs imported from Turkey tend to be past their best, so I go for *pan de higo*. But it's dangerously more-ish.'

Because his English was as idiomatic as her own, she took it for granted he would understand the expression.

'It doesn't appear to be doing any damage to your figure.' Switching to Spanish, he added, 'I'm sure all the somewhat overpadded ladies behind me have looked enviously at your slim waist.'

To her annoyance, Cally felt herself blushing. She had always thought of Italian and French as being more musical languages than Spanish, but when Nicolás spoke *castellano*, in that caressing tone of voice, it sent a quiver down her spine.

She was relieved when her father joined them. It was not until many days later that she remembered that Nicolás had not answered her question about his day's route.

For dinner that night, instead of serving a first course, Juanita and Cally handed round big dishes of hot and cold *tapas* including *barquetas de espárragos* which were boat-shaped pastry containers filled with parsley and chive sauce topped with asparagus tips.

'Mm…I'd like the recipe for these,' Cally heard Peggy

say to Nicolás. They were both eating *chorizo* puffs, she noticed.

'They're good, but they're seriously fattening I've heard,' she heard him answer.

Peggy gave a little shriek of dismay. 'Why did you have to tell me that? Still, men like a curvy woman, don't they?' The flirtatious look she gave him made Cally feel embarrassed for her.

'I don't think most of us are attracted by model girls' figures,' was his reply. Then Cally had to move out of earshot.

When everyone moved to the table, he sat next to her father, leaving Peggy to exercise her *femme fatale* manner on one of the other men. Cally sat at the other end of the table, as she had the night before, but this time with different neighbours. Fulfilling her role as hostess and watching to see that everyone was enjoying their food and had wine in their glasses prevented her from listening to more than an occasional snatch of the conversation at the far end of the table. But she did observe that her father was in what she thought of as his Expert on Everything mode, and Nicolás was listening but saying little himself.

When the meal was over and Juanita had gone home, the guests seemed inclined to stay up later than they had the night before. When she felt her absence for quarter of an hour wouldn't be noticed, Cally went to the office to pick up her email.

Every day she received an email news update from *The Bookseller*, a weekly magazine that was the bible of the British book trade. What she read in the latest update about the firm she worked for made her groan aloud.

Edmund & Burke sees sales and profits dive. The third-quarter figures will increase fears that E&B will be forced into a period of retrenchment by its US parent.

*Results released show that sales at E&B fell 7% in the
three months ended 30th September. The previous year's
figures had been bolstered by the inclusion of one of its
titles in the Oprah Book Club selection (see Media Watch
below).*

Cally scrolled down to the Media Watch section. What
she read made her even more depressed. According to a
report in the *Financial Times*, Edmund & Burke's parent
company would have to cut costs by two hundred million
dollars over the next twelve months. Inevitably drastic cuts
would have to be made by the UK subsidiary.

She read the update again. Then, too upset to open the
rest of the emails, none of which was important, she logged
off. For three or four minutes she sat slumped in the chair,
knowing that by the time she returned to London the imprint
she worked for would have been axed and her name would
have been added to the long list of editors made redundant
in recent years.

And where else, when publishing was awash with un-
employed editors and other publishing industry discards,
was she going to find another niche to suit her particular
talents?

Cally returned to the lounge only because she felt she ought
to be around in case anyone wanted more coffee or drinks.
She didn't join the cheerful group sitting on the comfortable
chairs and sofas, but slipped unobtrusively behind the bar
to be there if she was wanted but unnoticed if she wasn't.

A few minutes later, while she was pretending to read the
paper but thinking about the dire news from London,
Nicolás came over.

'Are you all right?' he said, as she looked up. 'When you
came back, you looked upset.'

'You imagined it,' she said lightly. 'I'm fine. Like another drink?'

'No, thanks. What I'd like is to go with you up to the roof terrace and talk about books. Will you come?'

'I can't. I'm on duty.'

'You've been on duty all evening. I'm sure your father can cope. Come on…let's get some fresh air,' he said persuasively.

At that moment Peggy gave a screech of raucous laughter that made Cally wince. Fleetingly, she saw the same pained expression on his face. Suddenly the thought of the peace and quiet of the terrace, with a congenial companion, was irresistible.

'All right,' she said. 'Why not?'

But even as she said it, several reasons why it wasn't a wise move occurred to her. She ignored them.

CHAPTER THREE

'DID you enjoy the roast lamb?' she asked, as she went up the stairs ahead of him.

'It was excellent…real home-cooking,' said Nicolás. 'In restaurants it's usually been cooked earlier and re-heated in the micro. It never tastes the same. This morning, you mentioned that a vegetarian rang up. Do you get many of them?'

'Not many, but we have a good repertoire of vegetarian dishes when they do come.'

'Did you go for a swim as you said you might?'

It was flattering that he remembered the details of their breakfast-time conversation in such detail.

'Yes, I enjoyed it…as long as I kept looking out to sea and not at the poor old coast which seems to have sprouted more villas and apartment blocks every time I go.'

'You don't go often?'

'Not very often. I used to be mad about swimming as a child, but it seems to be losing its allure. It takes forty minutes to get there and my mother's clapped-out old car has started to make worrying noises.'

'You haven't a car of your own.'

'I don't need one.' She didn't want to start explaining about living in London, especially now when her whole way of life there was hanging in the balance. 'Dad doesn't often go out at night so I have the use of his, which is newer and more reliable, if I want to go to a movie or wherever.'

'There isn't a steady boyfriend to take you about?'

'No,' said Cally. 'No, there isn't. Do you have a steady girlfriend?'

They had reached the top landing. As he had the night

before, Nicolás moved ahead of her to draw aside the fringe-like curtain. But before he did, he said, 'If I had, I shouldn't have suggested a tête-à-tête with you.'

'I don't see why having a girlfriend would debar you from friendly conversations with other women,' said Cally, as he moved the curtain out of her way.

'From friendly conversations—no. But are our reactions to each other purely friendly?' he asked, as he followed her onto the terrace.

Cally tensed. At that moment all thought of the doomsville email was swept from her mind as effectively as if she had looked across the *plana*, as the locals called the floor of the valley, and seen a spaceship landing there.

'What else could they be? You only arrived yesterday.'

'How long does it take to feel attracted to someone?'

Cally moved to the edge of the terrace and stood with her arms folded and her back to him. She didn't know what to say. She could deny that she was attracted to him. But would he believe her?

Before she had made up her mind how to respond, she felt his hands on her shoulders, gently but firmly turning her to face him.

'I don't think I did imagine that something had happened to upset you,' he said quietly. 'You came back into the lounge looking as pale as death. Can't you tell me about it? A trouble shared is a trouble halved, as my first English teacher used to say.'

He sounded so concerned and kind that, for a few mad seconds, she was tempted to lean against him and pour out all her anxiety. But then, as she stared at the top button of his shirt, Nicolás put the backs of his fingers under her chin and tilted her face up to his.

What happened then was outside all her previous experience. She forgot everything but an overwhelming desire to be in his arms and feel his lips on hers.

It would have happened. In those seconds it seemed inevitable. But then, from somewhere downstairs, they heard someone calling her name, the calls becoming louder and more urgent.

'Cally…Cally…where are you?'

'It's your father,' said Nicolás, stepping back and heading for the landing.

Pulling herself together, wondering what could require her urgent attention, she followed and heard Nicolás call down the staircase, 'Cally is up here.'

They met Douglas Haig as, puffing from unaccustomed exertion, he was about to start up the last flight.

'It's Fred…he's been taken ill. I think he may be having a heart attack.'

Nicolás's reaction was instantaneous. He shot down the staircase ahead of her. Hard on his heels, Cally said, 'I'll call an ambulance.'

'First let's make sure it's not indigestion,' he said, over his shoulder.

Two hours later, having followed the ambulance to the nearest hospital, and supported Peggy through the formalities of her husband's admission, they drove back to Valdecarrasca in Douglas Haig's car.

Cally had driven on the outward journey, but Nicolás insisted on driving on the return journey.

''You've had a long, tough day,' he said, holding out his hand for the car key.

She gave it to him, grateful for the unaccustomed solicitude, but hoping he wouldn't persist in trying to confirm that his hunch about her distress had been correct.

To her relief, he didn't attempt to have a conversation, but concentrated on driving an unfamiliar car on an unfamiliar and, once they had left the urban environs of the hospital, winding country road.

In the passenger seat, Cally relaxed. Out of the corner of her eye she watched his hands on the steering wheel and gear lever. She could have dealt with the emergency on her own but, when they found Fred collapsed in the lounge with the others crowding round him, had been happy to let Nicolás take charge.

He had done it so efficiently and knowledgeably that she had begun to wonder if he was a doctor. But if that were the case, surely he would have revealed his occupation to the staff at the hospital?

Peggy, whom Cally would have expected to become distraught and hysterical in any emergency situation, had been surprisingly calm. While they were waiting for the ambulance to arrive, she had changed her evening outfit for more sensible clothes and packed their belongings, leaving one suitcase behind and taking the other to the hospital where she was staying overnight.

When they were nearing the village, Cally said, 'I'm sorry this has happened the night before you go through the Barranc de L'Infern. What time are you meeting the others who are going through with you?'

'We're convening at nine at a bar called Oasis at the village of Benimaurell. Do you know it?'

'Only by name. I've never been there. How are you going to get there?'

'I'm being picked up at eight-fifteen.'

There being nowhere else for it, Douglas Haig had to keep his car in the village car park. Nicolás remembered the way without needing directions.

By this time Cally was feeling totally bushed. He seemed as clear-eyed and energised as he had been at breakfast. But presumably, whatever he did for a living, his job was not in jeopardy.

'Thank you for going with me,' she said, as they walked through the narrow, deserted streets between the car park and her parents' house. In the English village where her grandmother had lived, at this time of night the residents had either been in bed, or the blue glow of television screens had been visible through their curtains. Here the roll-down blinds called *persianas* concealed any signs of life from passersby. Nor did the façades of the houses give much clue to the size or comfort of their interiors.

'Glad to be of service,' said Nicolás. 'Not that you couldn't have managed perfectly well without me.'

'Perhaps...but I was grateful for your backup.'

When they entered the house, she was surprised to find that some of the others were still up.

'Go to bed, Cally,' said Nicolás, giving her a gentle push towards the stairs. 'I'll tell them as much as we know. Goodnight.'

She murmured goodnight and went wearily up the stairs.

Early next morning she downloaded an email from her publisher friend Nicola Russell.

Hi Cally

Things are not looking good at E&B. I have a sinking feeling that you're going to be in the same boat that I was when Richard came from the US to 'restructure' Barking & Dollis. But as that turned out to be all for the best in the long run, I shouldn't be too depressed if I were you. Often what look like disasters have a way of turning into opportunities.

If Richard or I could offer you a new home, we should be delighted to do so. But as you know we have both taken on board some casualties from the last wave of purges so, sadly, neither of us can come to the rescue. But you may be sure we have our ears close to the ground and, if we hear of anything suitable, will let you know at once.

I would telephone for a gossip, but don't want to call at an inconvenient moment when you're coping with guests. The beauty of email is that it doesn't intrude on people's lives the way the telephone does.

As soon as you get back, come to supper. Three heads are better than one in these situations.

Meanwhile, keep your chin up. Easy to say, I know, but I have been on the receiving end of the 'We're sorry, but...' message so can empathise better than those who haven't been axed.

Love and telepathic hugs from us both—Nicola

PS I hope your mother appreciates how lucky she is to have a daughter to hold the fort for her. Most twenty-somethings of my acquaintance ignore their parents, except when they want to make use of them. Richard thinks you're a Trojan, and so do I.

Comforted by Nicola's support, Cally took a quick look at the websites of two British book trade weeklies and at the online version of *Publishers Weekly*, bible of the US book trade. But none had any more news on the subject of most interest to her.

As he had the day before, Nicolás came down to breakfast early, but so did two other guests and she had no private conversation with him until he collected his packed lunch while she was in the kitchen.

'Have a good day. Take care,' she said.

'Thank you...I always do,' he said, with a smile.

Several times, during the day, she found herself worrying about him. Men had died in the Barranc de L'Infern. It was said that a shepherd had drowned there, after searching for a lost sheep, falling into a pool inside the ravine and being unable to clamber out because of the smoothness of the rock. More recently, two climbers had attempted to get through but one had fallen and been killed. His companion had been left hanging in his harness for several days until rescuers had found him.

It was true that many experienced rock-scramblers did negotiate the ravine safely. But some photographs Cally had seen made it look a sinister place, its fascination hard to fathom.

By all accounts, if anyone did have an accident, breaking an arm or a leg, it would be extremely difficult for their companions to get them out.

Nicolás did not think about Cally while he was in the Barranc. The nature of the terrain required all his concentration.

But after he and his companions had got through, there was more than an hour's walk back to where the car had been left. He thought about her then, wondering what had upset her the night before, and how she would have responded if he had kissed her.

In his early twenties, he had had an American girlfriend, but had never been on close terms with a British girl. Not that Cally was British in any practical sense. Toiling as a general factotum to her parents, she was completely unlike the ambitious, self-centred twentysomethings who worked, played and shopped in Madrid and other big cities in Europe and the US.

Last night, on the roof terrace, when he had tipped up her chin, preparatory to kissing her, the expression on her face had been a curious mixture of eagerness and uncertainty. It had not been the confident expression of a woman who knew she was beautiful and was accustomed to enjoying sex with selected partners.

Perhaps she didn't know she was beautiful. Because she didn't look like a model or a pop singer, the icons of female allure promoted by the media, she might not realise how much rarer and more lasting her kind of beauty was. Even in cheap chain store clothes, she had style. Dressed in the kind of clothes his sisters wore, she would be a knockout.

Nicolás was out to dinner that night. Cally gathered he was going to a booze-up with the guys he had spent the day with. As the rest of the guests had checked out, Juanita had a night off and Cally cooked supper for herself and her father.

Anticipating that Nicolás was likely to sleep late after a macho drinking session, Cally went out early for an aerobic walk on the *plana*. In London, during the summer months, she walked in the park near her studio flat. In winter she went to a gym. Here she had to adapt her walks to the other demands on her time.

Striding along the narrow lanes and dirt tracks between the small family-owned vineyards, she forced herself not to think of the catastrophe happening in London but to concentrate on the pleasures of the moment: the fresh air, the sunlight, the wide ring of sheltering mountains whose contours changed as the light changed.

On the other side of the valley, in the direction she was going at the moment, there was a small wooded hill whose trees had escaped the summer fires—usually caused by careless smokers or deliberately set by arsonists—that plagued many parts of Spain in the long hot summers.

She had heard that, hidden by the trees, there was a rather grand house which had been empty for decades. One day she meant to find out if the story was true, but there was seldom time to wander at will.

On the return stretch of the walk, when she was looking towards the village, her eye was caught by the house belonging to Cameron Fielding, a television reporter and Valdecarrasca's most famous inhabitant.

Neither Cally nor her parents had ever met him, but the day after her return she had run into a friend of his who also lived in the village. Mrs Dryden had told her that, to everyone's surprise, Fielding had fallen in love with the English widow who had looked after his garden.

Now they were married and living in Washington DC, leaving the house called La Higuera closed up. As told by Mrs Dryden, it was a romantic story of an unlikely pair of soul mates finally finding each other and being destined to live happily ever after.

Being happily married herself, Mrs Dryden was a believer in what, from Cally's perspective, was an unrealistic outcome. Even if she hadn't grown up with mismatched parents, the milieu she moved in, in London, was littered with broken or doomed-to-end-unhappily relationships.

Richard and Nicola were the only people she knew who were perfectly matched. Maybe Cameron Fielding and his former gardener were another. But in Cally's view the operative word was maybe.

She had finished the strenuous part of her walk, checking her pulse to make sure she had achieved the necessary acceleration, and was heading back to the village, when she heard someone running on the road behind her.

Expecting to see a German jogger with whom she sometimes exchanged a *'Bon día'*, the local form of *Buenos días*, she was surprised to see Nicolás catching her up.

'Good morning. I thought you would still be in bed after your night out,' she said as, slowing to a walk, he came abreast.

'Good morning. I was back by midnight. The others are climbing on the Peñon d'Ifach today, and late nights and climbing don't mix.'

'Aren't you going with them?'

'I have something else I want to do. Are you busy today? Would you have time to drive me somewhere?'

Against her better judgment, she found herself saying, 'I'm fairly free today, once I've got all the bedrooms sorted.'

'I can help you. When I was small, I was taught how to make my bed with proper hospital corners.'

'Really?' said Cally, smiling. 'You don't look at all the sort of person one would expect to know how to do that.'

'You shouldn't judge by appearances,' said Nicolás, also smiling. 'I have many unlikely skills. If you gave me a ball of wool and an old-fashioned wooden cotton reel with some fine nails stuck in one end, I could make you a long length of cord.'

'I know how to do that. My grandmother taught me when I was very small.'

'The world is full of *abuelas* with arcane skills they pass down to their grandchildren. Though perhaps that kind of grandmother is now an endangered species. She had time on her hands. Nobody has time on their hands any more,' he added sardonically.

'Not only that, I don't think today's children would be interested. They are far more sophisticated than I was at five or six.'

'Mostly they are what you call couch potatoes,' Nicolás said, with a shrug of broad brown shoulders. 'My nephews and nieces spend all their time glued to TV or playing games on their computers. God knows what sort of health problems they are stacking up for when they're adult.'

'Well, you're no couch potato,' said Cally. 'I looked round a few minutes ago, when I was checking my pulse rate, and there was no sign of you. I would certainly have spotted that yellow running top if you had been in view.'

'I know it's a horrible colour, but it shows up well in motorists' headlights if I'm running at night which I sometimes do to unwind after a difficult day.'

'It's a good colour on brown skin. It would only look

horrible on the lobster-pink skin you see at the beach in summertime. Why are your days sometimes difficult?' She was impatient to know what he did for a living.

'Actually they're not that bad…no worse than average,' he said. 'But I work in an office environment and I'm basically an outdoor person. Though I doubt if I should have been happier working on the land as everyone in these parts used to do,' he added dryly. 'It's back-breaking work, tending vines. Nobody wants to do it if they can do something easier.'

Cally decided that she wasn't going to press him about the exact nature of his work. He would either tell her or he wouldn't.

'Where is it you want me to drive you?' she asked.

'Oh…not far. About half an hour inland. Could we leave about one o'clock and come back about five? Would that be convenient?'

'Perfectly. But where are we going…and why?'

He gave her a teasing glance. 'Don't you like surprises?' Then, quickly, he added, 'Sorry…I was forgetting we haven't been introduced in the conventional sense. You're right to be wary of taking off into the blue with someone who walked in off the street.'

'That hadn't occurred to me,' said Cally. 'I went with you the other night without any worries.'

'It was an emergency. You didn't have time to think about it. Today is different. I should explain myself. I would like you to have lunch with me at a hotel I saw in the mountains yesterday. But perhaps you've been there already?'

'I've heard of the place you mean. I haven't been there, but some of our guests have. They were impressed. It's in a wonderful location and I gather the architecture is very sympathetic to the landscape.'

'I only saw it from a distance but, yes, it seemed so.'

'I'd like to come. Oh...' Her exclamation was caused by the sight of a Spanish hunting dog streaking towards them.

The dog—in shape like a greyhound and the colour of toffee—belonged to an elderly man who lived in the village. It was young and exuberant and a couple of times had collided with Cally, not meaning any harm but once nearly throwing her off balance and the second time grazing her thigh with the buckle on its collar. On other occasions its owner had shouted a command, making it race back to him. Today he was gazing in another direction and hadn't noticed it hurtling towards her and Nicolás.

When it was almost on them, he stepped in front of her and fended the dog off, engaging it in the kind of playful tussle that only people with total confidence in their rapport with animals attempted. Then with a wave of dismissal he sent it racing back to its master.

'He ought to keep it under better control. It could knock an old lady down, charging at her at that speed.'

'She would probably shout whatever it is that he shouts,' said Cally. 'I haven't mastered the words they yell at their dogs.'

'Dogs respond to a tone of voice. Have you never had a dog of your own?'

'No, I haven't. Have you?'

'When I was a boy. Not in Madrid. Cities and big dogs don't mix. I'm not keen on small dogs...lapdogs.'

They passed and exchanged polite greetings with the old man who looked with open curiosity at Cally's companion.

Back at the house, she had a quick shower before going down to lay the breakfast table. Nicolás came down soon afterwards and insisted on helping her. Compared with her father who was hopeless domestically, he was surprisingly competent.

He was chatting to her father when she slipped away to start sorting out the bedrooms. She had stripped the beds and washed all the sheets and pillowcases the day before, but not mopped the floors or remade the beds.

She was cleaning the shower room adjoining Peggy's and Fred's room when Nicolás put his head round the door.

'What can I do to help?'

Cally's first reaction was to say, 'Nothing, thanks. I can manage.' Then, for a reason she couldn't analyse, she said, 'You could make up the beds, if you would.'

'Right.' He disappeared.

A few minutes later she looked to see how he was getting on. One bed was already made up with its quilt on. He was making the other, dealing with it as efficiently as an experienced chambermaid.

Intent on his task he didn't notice her watching him. How odd, she thought. A Madrileño, working in an office environment—whatever that meant—who knew how to make a bed properly. According to her girlfriends, shaking up a duvet was the limit of their boyfriends' domestic skills.

She had left a mop and a bucket with a bowl compartment inside the door. To her astonishment, Nicolás began to use it as adeptly as if he spent his life mopping floors.

'Where on earth did you learn to do that?' she asked, from the inner doorway.

He straightened. 'I grew up in an old house where everything was done the old-fashioned way. But I don't understand why you're still using this thing rather than a modern mop with a foam rubber pad.'

'I like the traditional methods,' she said lightly. The real reason was that her mother's succession of domestic helps preferred to do things the way their mothers had done them. In rural Spain, the young were enthusiasts for new, effort-saving ways, but many of the middle-aged and elderly clung to the habits of a lifetime.

'Shall I take over?' she suggested.

'No, I'll finish here. You go and start on the next room. That way we'll get it done sooner.'

Cally heard the telephone ringing. She ran down the stairs to answer it. She was kept on the line for some time.

In her absence, Nicolás finished mopping the floor, wondering as he did so how his friends and family would react if they could see him engaged in this unlikely task.

Why *was* he doing it? he asked himself.

Was it for the amusement of assuming a persona far removed from his usual self? Was it because he was hoping to resume the rooftop tête-à-tête interrupted by her father's call for help?

His thoughts switched to Douglas Haig who reminded him of his own uncle, Tio Francesco, a man of considerable charm, like Cally's father, but also a hopeless sot until he had been dried out at an expensive clinic.

It seemed unlikely that any of the *casas rurales*, and certainly not this one, made more than a reasonable living for their owners. Certainly the profits here would not stretch to the fees of a clinic where Mr Haig could be weaned off the bottle.

But it seemed grossly unfair that Cally should have to waste her life helping to prop up her parents. Perhaps she was devoted to her mother. Or perhaps her mother, like his own, was what he thought of as a 'user': someone with no compunction about manipulating others to serve their convenience.

Before they set out for the hotel, Cally changed into black linen trousers and a white cotton shirt, with a silk-and-linen-mix camel-coloured sweater to slip on if it were cooler at a higher altitude. Tortoiseshell earrings, a tortoiseshell bangle and several unusual rings, picked up in *rastros* here and street markets in London, completed a 'look' she hoped would pass muster whether the hotel's clientele was casual or sophisticated.

Nicolás was sitting in one of the cane chairs in the entrance lobby, reading a copy of the English-language magazine *Valencia Life* that someone had left behind, when she reached the ground floor. He rose, put the magazine aside, and gave her a comprehensive appraisal.

'You look as if you should be working in the fashion industry,' he said.

'Thank you. You look good too—but not as if you might work in the fashion industry,' she added, smiling.

His grin made creases in his cheeks that she found disturbingly sexy. 'I should hope not. Are we ready to go?'

'Just as soon as I've said goodbye to my father.'

'He's in the office.'

Cally put her head round the door. 'I'm just off, Dad.'

He was studying a telephone bill that must have arrived while she was upstairs. He glanced up and gave the grunt that signalled he was not pleased at being left in charge.

'See you later,' Cally said equably, not showing her irritation at his inveterate selfishness. At moments like this she could understand why he drove her mother barmy. But then her mother wasn't easy to live with either.

Putting them both firmly out of her mind, she rejoined Nicolás. 'Let's go.'

On the way to the car park they passed a group of women gossiping on a street corner. Cally knew them only by sight but, within the boundaries of the village, everyone exchanged polite greetings.

When they looked round to see who was passing, Nicolás said good morning to them. Immediately, and without exception, every woman in the group reacted to being addressed by a good-looking man with an air about him that they seemed to recognise in the way that Juanita had.

His greeting was returned with gracious smiles and a

sparkle that made it easier to visualise how they had looked when they were Cally's age.

'My stock will have gone up no end,' she said dryly.

Nicolás made no comment on that. 'Do you mix with the village people much?'

'Not really...except with Juanita. The rest are always pleasant and friendly, but it's difficult for foreigners to establish any kind of intimacy. I know one or two foreign children who have grown up here, but they don't get invited into their Spanish friends' homes as they would in America or England. Different countries...different ways.'

'Country people are always clannish.'

'It's surprising the Spanish don't seem to resent this extraordinary invasion of their country by hordes of Americans, Brits, Scandinavians, Germans and all the other nationalities whose winter climate at home drives them to come here.'

'The foreigners have brought prosperity to a land that, two generations ago, was still very poor,' said Nicolás. 'Spain wouldn't be enjoying her present affluence were it not for all the incomers. The Spanish are realists. It's better to put up with incomers than to be forced to emigrate, as many had to after our Civil War left this country in a bad way.'

Because it offered more leg room for someone of his height, Cally, who had keys to both, decided to use her father's car rather than her mother's.

As they headed west, deeper into the mountains, she was keenly aware of the broad shoulder close to her own and the long muscular thigh on the other side of the gear lever. She drove more slowly and carefully than she had the other night when she was following the ambulance. Driving in Spain had taught her to be wary of oncoming vehicles whose drivers might be holding a cellphone in one hand and gesticulating with the other.

It was half-past one when they reached their destination; still on the early side by Spanish standards, but already several tables in the dining room were occupied by foreigners who had finished their starters and were eating their main course.

'Let's have a drink on the terrace, shall we?' said Nicolás. 'I'll drive back so you don't need to watch your alcohol intake. What would you like to drink?'

Cally could think of several women she had met at Young Publishers meetings who, super-sensitive to the smallest sign of a man being patronising, would have taken umbrage at that remark. She knew they would despise her for it, but the fact was that she rather liked having responsibility taken off her shoulders. One could have enough of being responsible.

'A glass of white wine, please.'

Being driven back, several hours later, she realised it was a long time since she had enjoyed herself as much as she had today.

Lunching in good restaurants was not a new experience. She had done it many times in London, with her authors. Good food and attentive service were not novelties to her. But today she had been the guest rather than the host because, when the bill was presented and she had suggested they go Dutch, Nicolás had said firmly that he would not hear of it. She had sensed that he would be seriously offended if she argued.

'I can't remember when I last laughed so much. You are very good company,' she told him, on the way back. She knew that the wine she had drunk had loosened her tongue a little, but when he had been such an amusing companion why shouldn't she pay him a compliment?

'I'm glad you've enjoyed it. I've had a good time too.

We get on well,' he said, taking his eyes off the road for a moment to give her that pulse-quickening smile.

Cally made a murmur of agreement. Only then did it dawn on her that, from the time they arrived, she hadn't given a thought to the situation in London or the bleak outlook for the future. Nor did she want to think about them now. This afternoon had been a holiday from real life and she didn't want it to end. But end it must because, by the time they got back, two more guests would have arrived.

Nicolás and Cally did not join the newcomers and her father at the table that evening. Nicolás asked if he could use the desk in the office to do some writing on his computer and later he came to the bar and had a smoked salmon and rye bread sandwich. Cally wasn't hungry. She had a tangerine and, perhaps unwisely, another glass of wine when Nicolás had one. But he had drunk less at lunchtime.

The Dutch couple, perhaps disappointed to find themselves the only visitors—they probably assumed that Nicolás was Cally's Spanish boyfriend—went to bed early. Mr Haig, who had a TV set in the room he shared with his wife, went upstairs to watch football, one of the few interests he shared with the men of his adopted country.

'Alone at last,' said Nicolás, when the sound of her father's footsteps mounting the staircase had died away. 'Come and sit on the sofa with me and let's continue our discussion on Life and Literature.'

There was a glint in his eyes that warned Cally he had more than a discussion in mind. She knew that she ought to make some excuse about having things to do, but the truth was that she wanted to sit on the sofa with him.

Aware that she was being foolish, but unable to resist the power of his attraction for her, she went round to his side of the bar. Nicolás had risen from the bar stool. He took her hand and led her towards the sofa. The feel of his fingers enclosing hers sent a spasm of pleasure right to the top of her arm.

'Where shall we start?' he said, as they sat down. 'Do you ever go to *Arts & Letters Daily*?'

In the context of what she judged to be his intentions, the question astonished her. 'It's my number one favourite website. I love it. The look of it…the content…everything.'

'I like it too,' he said. 'I'd say it was the most consistently interesting site on the web, at least for bookish people like ourselves.' And then he smiled and, letting go of her hand, put his arm round her. 'But perhaps we should discuss it tomorrow. Tonight I would rather kiss you.' Which he proceeded to do.

It was a long time since Cally had been kissed; so long that she had almost forgotten how it felt to have a large hand cupping the back of her head and warm lips exploring her face. She closed her eyes and relaxed into his embrace, her heart thudding against her ribs as she waited for the moment when his lips would find hers.

When they did, she found that being kissed by Nicolás in real life beat everything she had imagined while lying in bed after the nearly-but-not-quite kiss on the roof terrace.

All the kisses in her past from the inexpert kisses of teenage Spanish boys to the kisses of her only serious relationship faded into insignificance compared with the deep excitement this man's kiss was arousing in her.

For the first time she understood what wanting a man really meant. As his arms tightened round her, she slid her arms round his neck and melted against him.

How long it lasted, she had no idea. It seemed to go on for ever yet, when he lifted his head, to have ended far too soon.

When she opened her eyes, he was looking intently at

her, his dark eyes brilliant with desire. 'I think we are both too old for necking on a sofa,' he said huskily. 'Let's go somewhere more comfortable and more private.' He stood up, drawing her with him. 'My room…or yours?'

CHAPTER FOUR

CALLY had often watched para-gliders soaring above the valley on the air currents generated by the mountains. Occasionally one of them would suddenly plummet downwards. Nicolás's question made her feel as if something similar were happening to her.

Pulling herself together—or as much together as she could manage in the circumstances—she said, 'Nicolás... I'm sorry...I think we have our wires crossed. Wanting to kiss you doesn't mean I'm ready to go to bed with you.'

When he didn't react, she added, 'I know many people do...but I think it's a mistake. I—I like you enormously, and I think we have lots in common. But you only arrived here three days ago, and that's not long enough to switch from being strangers to lovers.'

While she was speaking, Nicolás had released his hold on her and made a space between them.

'Very well...if that's how you feel,' he said evenly. 'In that case we had better go to bed—separately. I won't say "sleep well" because I don't think either of us is likely to do that. Goodnight, Cally.'

'Goodnight.' She watched him walk away, finding it hard to believe that a few moments earlier her elbows had been resting on those broad shoulders and one of her hands had been stroking the nape of his neck.

When he had gone, she went to the wicket door and locked it. Then she turned off all the downstairs lights and went up to her room.

She knew she had made the right decision: that sleeping

with him, so soon, would have damaged her self-respect and violated all the rules she had made for herself.

Other people did it. Other people treated sex as if it were no big deal, no more important than any of life's other physical pleasures…eating, drinking, sun-bathing, swimming, dancing. But to Cally it *was* more important. She felt that making love was something she only wanted to share with someone so special that, beside him, all other men paled into insignificance. Someone who felt the same way about her.

She didn't doubt for a moment that making love with Nicolás would have been wonderful. That a night in his arms would have obliterated the memory of her first disappointing experience of sex.

But for him, she felt sure, she was just an addition to a long line of women who had taken his fancy. He might like her, but he would forget her as soon as he left Valdecarrasca. While she, had she let him share her bed, or shared his, would have remembered him always. And was likely to do that anyway.

When the church clock struck midnight, Nicolás was still awake, lying on his back in the moonlight, thinking about the girl who, if he had had his way, would be lying beside him.

The urgent need that her pliant body and soft lips had aroused in him earlier had ebbed now. He could view what had happened dispassionately. Cally was the first woman who had ever said no to him. Surprisingly, he found himself admiring her strength of will. She wanted him as much as he wanted her. He was sure of that. But she hadn't been out of control, incapable of resisting the demands of her senses.

In his heart he knew she was right. To advance from being strangers to lovers in three days *was* too fast, unless there were exceptional circumstances such as a war when, knowing they might be killed, people grabbed everything life had to offer with both hands.

But these were not exceptional circumstances and clearly Cally was someone who had worked out a set of principles and was determined to stick to them however strongly her body conspired against her.

In his world, people who made their own rules, regardless of peer pressure, were increasingly rare. Most women were like sheep, allowing themselves to be conned into wearing ridiculous fashions designed by men with no interest in the opposite sex except to profit from their gullibility. Women with voluptuous figures starved themselves in an effort to emulate twig-thin fashion models. Other women paid insane amounts of money to have their hair frizzed and fuzzed into bizarre styles. Many were also being conned into having their faces and bodies improved by cosmetic surgery. From a man's point of view, all these were aberrations. What made a woman attractive was the warmth of her personality, her sense of humour, her sympathy for life's unfortunates.

As far as he could tell, Cally's only flaw was her failure to escape from her parents' influence, her willingness to adapt her life to their needs rather than her own. Her conversation over lunch had confirmed that she had a keen and questing intelligence, that her interests went far beyond the boundaries of the narrow world of Valdecarrasca and its environs.

She ought to be holding down a demanding job, not wasting her time propping up a business that her parents could run by themselves if they had to.

On this thought, he turned on his side and was soon asleep.

Next morning Cally expected Nicolás's manner towards her to be markedly cool. No man liked being rejected. She had not forgotten the furious resentment aroused when she had ended an affair with someone far less good-looking and personable than the Madrileño.

It seemed not only possible but likely that Nicolás had never been turned down before, and that would intensify his ire.

So it was with surprise and relief that she found, when he came down to breakfast, that he gave no sign of being put out and was as cheerful and pleasant as he had been before last night's abortive embrace.

After breakfast, he went out for the day, but didn't say where he was going and she didn't like to ask.

Late that afternoon, returning to the *casa rural*, Nicolás met Juanita coming out of the *farmacia*.

'I hear you took Cally to lunch at the hotel near Benimaurell,' she said, after greeting him. 'I didn't hear it from her. I have a cousin who lives in that village. He's met her. He recognised her as you drove through. His wife telephoned me to ask who you were.'

'News travels fast around here,' said Nicolás, amused.

'It does Cally good to relax. She works too hard,' said Juanita. She did not mention where the English girl did most of her work. If she hadn't told the Madrileño about her job in London, so much the better. It was Juanita's opinion that even young men were getting fed up with girls who were too independent. As they always had, and always would, men wanted a woman who would be a good wife and mother.

What Cally needed was a husband. Tomas, the handsome young fellow who came to the village every week delivering full gas bottles and collecting the empties, he had his eye on her. But he was a working man and always would be, not a toff like the Madrileño.

Juanita began to extol Cally's virtues: her patience, her good humour, the way she could buy something cheap from a market stall and make it look as if it had come from an expensive shop in Valencia or Alicante.

Nicolás, who had been targeted by match-makers before, recognised Juanita's motive for praising Cally and was even more amused. He wondered how the cook would react if he confided to her that he had already attempted to get Cally to share his bed. She would profess to be shocked, but it was possible that her own marriage had been the result of illicit couplings.

Despite their tut-tutting about the deterioration in manners and morals among today's young people, their parents and grandparents had not always obeyed the stricter codes in place when they were young. Human nature did not change, and he wouldn't mind betting that quite a few of the old boys who sat gossiping in the *plaza mayor*, and the portly housewives coming and going with their baskets and bread bags, had been conceived before their parents were married in the village church.

'When is Señora Haig expected back?' he asked.

Juanita told him, adding, 'She's visiting her friend in England. She'll come back with a cold. She always catches a cold when she goes there. Thank goodness I don't have to live in that terrible climate. No wonder so many of them come to Spain when they retire. It's bad enough getting old without having to put up with endless rain and cold weather for months on end.'

'English weather isn't always bad, and they have very comfortable houses.'

'You've been there, have you?'

'Several times. I have friends in England.'

'Spain is the best place to live, and this is the best part of Spain,' said Juanita with conviction.

'It certainly has a lot to recommend it,' Nicolás said tactfully. A cosmopolitan himself, he was accustomed to his compatriots' fierce devotion to their own particular region and its customs and cuisine, which they always considered superior to those of all other regions.

In the evening two Spanish representatives checked in for an overnight stay and the three men had a long chat. Listening to snatches of it, Cally noticed that, although the reps talked freely about themselves and their jobs, Nicolás said almost nothing about himself or his occupation.

All day she had been picking up email every two hours, each time expecting to download a redundancy notice. But although corporate publishers were famous for the ruthlessness of their dismissals, and would not feel bound to wait for an employee to return from holiday before sacking her, the email she dreaded did not come and she went to bed no wiser than when she got up.

But she had to admit to herself that it hadn't been only her job that had been on her mind. A lot of her thoughts had been about Nicolás: how much longer he intended to stay, whether he had written her off or would try to kiss her again, whether in six months' time she would regret turning him down.

Cally's first intimation that Nicolás had come to Valdecarrasca for a purpose he had not disclosed to her, and that was very different from his apparent reason, came on the way back from a visit to a produce market in a larger village.

She was driving home when she saw, returning on foot, a woman laden with carrier bags whom she knew by sight but not by name. Cally stopped to give her a lift.

After some general conversation, her passenger said, 'You've heard about the hotel, I expect.'

'What hotel is that?' asked Cally.

'I'm surprised you haven't heard about it when the man in charge has been staying at your place. But I suppose he thought it wouldn't do to mention it. I mean it's not going to be good for your business, is it?' said the woman, in a sympathetic tone.

'Where did you hear this rumour?' Cally asked.

'It's not a rumour, my dear. They were seen together at the house…the old house across the valley—' with a wave of the hand in the direction of the wooded knoll on the far side of the *plana*. 'The man who is staying with you, and another man who is an architect…quite a famous architect. The last hotel he designed won a prize. He was interviewed on TV. I didn't see him myself, but a lot of people did. It's the talk of the village. You can't run a hotel without staff, can you? They'll be looking for people to work there. So it won't help your business, but it will bring opportunities for other people.'

Cally listened, aghast. She felt as if, without any warning, someone had punched her in the stomach.

'It can't be the talk of the village,' she said. 'If it were Juanita who cooks for us would have heard about it. Who is the person who's supposed to have seen this famous architect over there?'

'It was old Diego Perez. He wanders about all over the place. They didn't see him but he saw them. He recognised them both…one from the television, and the other from seeing him about the village these past few days. The fellow who is staying with you had a key to the main door. Diego saw him unlock it. He must be the agent for the owners.'

Cally was beginning to recover from the initial shock. 'Who are the owners?'

'I don't know who owns it now. Most likely some property developer,' said her passenger. 'But if you want to know about the people who used to own it, the person to talk to is Dolores Martinez's grandmother. She's in her nineties and doesn't go out any more, but her mind is still clear so I've heard. Long ago she worked at that house as a kitchen maid.'

By this time they were back at the village where the older woman got out, retrieved her shopping from the back seat, thanked Cally and said goodbye. No doubt it would not be long before another snippet of information was circulating on the village grapevine: the fact that the English girl whose parents owned the *casa rural* had had no idea that the Madrileño staying there was a snake in the grass, Cally thought angrily.

She could hardly wait for Nicolás to come back from his day's activities so that she could confront him with his infamous conduct. Indeed she was strongly tempted to go to his room, stuff his belongings into a bin bag and dump them outside the front door with a curt note informing him he was no longer welcome.

Then she remembered that he had yet to pay his bill. It would be more prudent to insist on settlement of what he owed to date before telling him what she thought of him.

She had printed out his account ready to give him and was sitting, bolt upright and tense, on one of the bar stools, waiting to present it to him, when he came in.

Cally stepped down from the stool, inwardly trembling, outwardly calm. Ignoring his friendly, 'Hi…how are you?' she said coldly, 'Good evening. It's come to my ears that you are not here on holiday, as we thought…that you're involved in the restoration of a property on the other side of the valley, for business purposes. Is that information correct?'

Nicolás had taken off his backpack before he entered the building. Now he propped it against a chair and regarded her with an expression she could not interpret.

'Yes, it's true,' he agreed. 'But I wasn't aware that busi-

ness people were *persona non grata*. You've had a couple
of reps here since I arrived.'

'That's entirely different. You can't seriously expect us
to welcome someone whose activities will undermine our
livelihood. I'm afraid I must ask you to leave—immediately.
This is your bill.' She held it out to him.

Nicolás moved forward and took it, his dark gaze still
locked with hers. 'Why will my project undermine your
livelihood?' he asked.

Cally began to lose her cool. 'If you can't see that, you
want your brains tested. A large hotel a couple of kilometres
away is going to kill us stone dead. It may bring some
employment, but it certainly won't bring tranquillity. But
why should you care if this valley is ruined like so much
of the coast has been ruined? You don't have to live here.
You'll go back to Madrid. It's we who will have to suffer
the consequences.'

As he continued to fix her with that enigmatic stare, she
was torn between wanting to continue her rant and feeling
that it would be wiser to hold her tongue.

Eventually he said, 'Whatever I do, or don't do, all the
areas close to the airports and the *autopista* are going to
change dramatically in the next ten years. Nothing can alter
that. I think you must resign yourself to it.' He glanced
down at the bill. 'Can I pay this by Visa?'

'Certainly.'

He reached into the back pocket of his jeans for his wallet, found the credit card and offered it to her. 'You can be
dealing with that while I go up and clear my room.' He
picked up his pack and disappeared up the stairs.

Putting his card through the machine, Cally felt a twinge
of unease about ejecting him at this time of day instead of
requesting he leave first thing tomorrow. Still, he could easily hitch a lift to the nearest sizeable town where there was
at least one *hostal*.

She knew that the anger she felt was exacerbated by the fact that he had made what she now saw as an opportunistic pass at her, although at the time she had convinced herself that he had been motivated by tenderness as well as lust.

For personal reasons, she wanted him out of her sight and the sooner the better.

Within ten minutes she heard him coming downstairs.

He came to the bar, signed the slip and said, 'I've put the books I borrowed back where I found them. In case, for any reason, you should want to get in touch with me, I'll give you my email address.'

He put his part of the Visa slip in his wallet and extracted a card which he put on the counter followed by a twenty-euro note.

'You forgot to include my Internet use while I've been here. I think that should cover it.'

'It's too much.'

He shrugged. 'Anything over you can put in the charity box. Goodbye, Cally. I won't offer you my hand. I'm sure you don't want to shake hands with someone you obviously despise.' His smile mocked her hostile expression.

He walked out of the house and out, she hoped, of her life.

Going upstairs to strip his bed, Cally would have been less sanguine on that score had she known that Nicolás wasn't on his way out of the village but was knocking on Juanita's door.

After the Spanish woman had invited him into her house, he said, '*Señora*, I am thinking of staying in Valdecarrasca for some time—but not at the *casa rural* where the accommodation is good but not suitable for a long stay. Do you know of any houses to rent in the village, or near it?'

Juanita looked thoughtful. After a pause, she said, 'I've heard that La Higuera can be rented, but it's one of the finest houses in the village and is sure to be expensive. It depends what you can afford.'

'Where is La Higuera?'

'It's on the other side of the village. It belongs to an Englishman who works in television. He's famous, so they say. If you're interested, you will have to talk to Señora Dryden. She is also English, but her husband is an American. If you like, I'll take you to their house and introduce you.'

'You are very kind.'

'It's no trouble. May I ask why you want to spend longer in such a small, unimportant place as Valdecarrasca?'

'The village is charming. I find it very much to my liking.' Nicolás knew the conclusion she would draw—at least until Cally told her she had thrown him out.

The door of the Drydens' house was opened by an elderly man wearing a cotton shirt with a silhouette of a polo-player embroidered on the chest. Nicolás recognised it as the logo of an American designer who specialised in the 'old money' look.

He waited for Juanita to present him.

'Señor Dryden, this young man has been staying at the *casa rural* but now he would like to rent a house and I thought perhaps La Higuera might suit him. Señor Llorca is from Madrid.'

The two men shook hands, the elder giving the younger a shrewd appraisal. 'You had better come in and talk to my wife,' he said. 'Will you take a glass of wine with us, *señora*?'

Although visibly gratified by the invitation, Juanita declined on the grounds of having things to do.

A few moments later Nicolás was ushered into a large living room where a woman a few years younger than the owner of the house was sitting on a comfortable sofa drinking what looked like Campari and soda.

'Leonora, this is Señor Llorca who is looking for a house to rent... Señor Llorca, my wife.'

Mrs Dryden rose and greeted him pleasantly in Spanish. 'We know of a house to rent but it is rather large for one person...or will there be others joining you?'

Switching to English, Nicolás said, 'It's possible I might have visits from friends, but mainly I shall be on my own. But I'm used to a good deal of space. The size of house, provided it's comfortable, is immaterial.'

He saw their brief exchange of glances—the silent communication of people who had known each other a long time and could read each other's mind—and knew that his fluent English and, even more, his accent had reassured them. They were of the generation and type who tended to feel more at ease with people from their own milieu whereas he, despite or perhaps because of his origins, was comfortable in any company.

'What would you like to drink?' asked his host. 'Gin and tonic? Wine?'

'Gin and tonic would be excellent. Ice but no lemon, please.'

'Do sit down.' Mrs Dryden indicated a large armchair set at right angles to the sofa where she was sitting. 'What brings you to this part of Spain?'

Half an hour later, Nicolás said goodbye, leaving his card with them and taking the email address of the owner of La Higuera.

From the telephone box in the *plaza mayor* he rang for a taxi to take him to Alicante. Then he went into a nearby bar to drink coffee and read the paper until the taxi arrived.

In her living room, Mrs Dryden was poring over a copy of the *Almanach de Gotha* which her husband, knowing her

interest in the complex relationships of European royalty
and nobility, had given her as a birthday present.

'I thought so,' she exclaimed triumphantly, beckoning her
husband to come and see what she had found.

When he was sitting beside her, she moved the book from
her lap to his and indicated the entry she wanted him to
read. 'I'm sure that's who he is—not plain Señor Nicolás
Llorca but His Excellency El Conde Nicolás Llorca,
younger son of the Duquesa de Baltasar.'

Todd Dryden read the entry. 'You may be right. He certainly has an air of distinction about him. But if he is a
Grandee, I don't think he'll want it advertised. If it got to
Mrs Haig's ears, she would shout it from the housetops of
course. How that couple produced such a sensible, intelligent daughter is a mystery to me.'

'My dear Todd, I have never been a blabbermouth, and
my interest in the Spanish aristocracy has nothing to do with
snobbery,' his wife retorted. 'I should be equally interested
in the family trees of the village people if they had been
recorded.' After a pause, she added, 'If and when we see
him again, I shall ask him if he is who I think he is. But
even if he isn't, he's still a very likeable young man, didn't
you think?'

'He has very good manners,' said her husband. 'But
whether his character matches them, who can say? There've
been plenty of rogues who were charm personified. Llorca's
looks will endear him to most women, but looks can be very
deceptive.'

'You have a suspicious mind,' said Leonora. 'You never
trust anyone till you've known them for years.'

Cally returned to London on a Sunday. The following afternoon she was summoned to the company's boardroom
and informed that her services were no longer required. It
was not as brutal a shock as it had been for her friend Nicola

Russell who had not expected to be sacked. Cally had been prepared for the axe to fall.

She did not return to her desk but went back to the small house in Chelsea where she and Deborah, who worked behind the scenes in TV, had bedsits and shared a bathroom while the rest of the house was occupied by its owner, Olivia, a literary agent who needed lodgers in order to pay her mortgage.

Olivia and Deborah were full of sympathy for Cally's predicament. The three of them sat up late, talking and drinking wine.

For the next two weeks, Cally networked. She had several meals with the Russells and knew they would do their utmost to help relocate her. But it was a period when the market was difficult, no one was expanding and there were many people, some better qualified than herself, competing for every publishing vacancy that came up.

One evening, after yet another day of pouring rain, she decided she might just as well go back to Valdecarrasca for a while. She found a cheap flight on the Internet, booked it and rang her mother to say she was coming and would catch the bus that, from Alicante bus station, passed through a town on the N322 which was only a short run from the village.

When Cally climbed down from the bus, she couldn't see either of her parents' cars parked nearby. Fortunately there was a bar close to the bus stop. She went in and ordered a coffee, wondering why, when she was habitually punctual and often early for appointments, her parents were invariably late.

Nearly a quarter of an hour later, she saw her mother's car pulling into a parking space. Having already paid for the coffee, Cally went out to join her.

'Sorry I'm late. It's been non-stop today,' said Mrs Haig,

as her daughter got into the car. After they exchanged kisses on both cheeks, she said, 'We weren't expecting to see you again so soon. Is everything all right?'

'No,' said Cally. 'I've lost my job.' She spoke matter-of-factly but, for a moment, she longed for her grandmother with whom she could have burst into tears and had a good howl.

'Oh, dear,' said Mrs Haig, frowning. 'Do you think you'll be out of work long?'

'I don't know. The prospects aren't good. I may have to do something different. I can keep an eye on the job market as easily from here as there. At least here I can give you a hand. That's better than watching the rain in London.'

'But what about your rent?' said her mother. 'How will you pay it if you're not earning?'

'They gave me a golden handshake. I can survive for six months. Don't worry about it, Mum. It's a matter of what's called regrouping. I'm not going to be a strain on your budget. I just need a week or two to rethink my future in case I can't get another post as an editor.'

'You'd be welcome to stay here permanently—if the business would support all three of us. Unfortunately it won't and, once the hotel on the other side of the valley gets going, it may not support the two of us,' Mrs Haig said gloomily.

They were halfway back to the village before she said, 'Oh, I nearly forgot. You've been asked out tonight. After you rang to say you were coming, I had a call from Mrs Dryden. She's giving a dinner party for some Spanish artist who doesn't speak English, so the guests have to speak Spanish. Bloody cheek to ring up at the last moment, if you ask me. But I said I'd get you to call her as soon as you arrived. I suppose one of her guests has dropped out at the last moment and she's clutching at straws. The Drydens' parties are good, so I've heard. Not that we've ever been asked.' She glanced at her daughter. 'If you don't want to go, you can easily make an excuse.'

'I'll think about it,' said Cally. The invitation puzzled her. Mrs Dryden had always been friendly when they met in the village, but she and her husband socialised with their own age group. Why should they want to invite someone of her generation? Whatever their reason, she had always been curious about the inside of their house, and going to a party would be better than spending the evening worrying about the future.

In Spain Cally rarely used any cosmetics apart from sunscreen and lipstick. But that evening, having rung Leonora Dryden and accepted the last-minute invitation, she spent half an hour putting on what she thought of as her book-launch-party face. Luckily she had some evening separates in her wardrobe, brought south the year before when her parents had been fully booked for the Christmas holiday period and she had needed to dress up a bit more than usual at night.

The black silk-velvet trousers were classics inherited from Deborah who was a fashion victim and never wore anything for more than a season. The black lace top might be considered a trifle *décolleté* by the stuffier sort of older person, but the Drydens did not have the reputation of being stuffy and anyway she was in a what-the-hell mood. At the last moment she decided to add a little black sequinned beret bought on a weekend in Paris. A black pashmina shawl, bought when pashminas were coming down from the luxury price bracket to more affordable levels, would hide her *décolletage* from anyone she passed on her way to the party. The beret would cause enough comment without a display of cleavage.

Predictably, her mother liked her outfit, but her father looked disapproving. He didn't object to the girls in skimpy, clinging outfits who postured and pouted on Spanish TV shows, she had noticed. But he didn't want his daughter to look sexy and most of the time she didn't. Tonight she was feeling a rare urge to cut a dash.

The sequinned beret triggered a fit of the giggles among a group of village children she passed after leaving the house. Further on an old man who knew her by sight stared as if he were seeing a stranger. As they exchanged good evenings, he stopped to watch her pass. Cally couldn't resist giving her hips an extra swing for his benefit. Before turning the corner into the next street, she looked back. The old man was still staring after her. She gave him a saucy wave. If I'm feeling like this now, after a couple of drinks I'll be ready to dance on the table, she thought, with a grin.

The Drydens' front door was opened by a girl in a white blouse and black skirt who asked if Cally would like to leave her wrap with her, and then, indicating a staircase, said the party was taking place upstairs.

At the top of the stairs was a landing with an open door giving a view of a large room lit by shaded table lamps and ceiling spotlights beamed onto paintings. As she was hovering on the threshold, admiring the book-filled alcoves, the comfortable sofas and beautiful oriental rugs spread on the rustic-tiled floor, her hostess came to welcome her.

'Miss Haig…how kind of you to come at such short notice. One of our guests does speak English, but the others don't and it's terribly hard to find foreigners who are comfortable speaking Spanish. I've heard that you speak Valenciano as well. First, let me get you a drink, and then you must meet some of the others.' She swept Cally to a side table being used as a bar and then, when her guest had a glass of white wine in her hand, started the introductions.

Cally had never found meeting strangers a problem and was pleasantly surprised to discover that not all the other guests were in the Drydens' age group. The first couple she met were in their early forties, the husband a doctor and his wife an amateur artist who had met Leonora Dryden at painting classes given by a professional.

She was chatting to them, and had just helped herself to an olive from a tray of nibbles offered by a waiter, when she saw her companions looking past her towards the door. What had attracted their attention was the arrival of a woman in a vivid red dress. She was escorted by a small rotund man.

Behind him was another, taller man. It took Cally a moment to register that she knew him because he looked so different wearing an elegant city suit with an immaculate shirt and a discreet silk tie.

Always a commanding presence by virtue of his height and build, tonight Nicolás Llorca looked like the kind of man who flew round the world in a private jet, spent his life making decisions, and exacted high levels of excellence from everyone under his dominion.

What was he doing here? she wondered. And how was he going to react when he recognised the wearer of the sequinned beret as the woman who, not long ago, had told him to get lost?

CHAPTER FIVE

WHILE the people who had arrived ahead of him were being welcomed by Todd Dryden, Nicolás was greeted by his hostess. Watching him kiss her hand, Cally felt a catch in her throat.

The graceful way he performed the gesture conjured up earlier times when it had been a customary act of homage by chivalrous men to beautiful women. She wondered if women like Mrs Dryden felt a pang of regret for their lost youth when they talked to someone as dynamic and virile as Nicolás. But presumably, forty years ago, Mr Dryden had been equally gorgeous.

As she realised that seeing Nicolás again had reactivated all the feelings she had had before discovering his duplicity, she pulled herself together, determined not to succumb to his charm a second time. Not that, after the way she had upbraided him, he was likely to waste any charm on her tonight. Hopefully they wouldn't have much contact. It was even possible that, in a party this size—she estimated there were now about twenty-four people in the room—they might have no contact at all.

Whether it was going to be the kind of party where people ate a series of *tapas* standing up, or slightly more substantial lap-food wherever they could find a perch, there was no way of knowing.

Having been up since six and eaten little since breakfast—the snack served on the plane had been typical economy flight fare—Cally was beginning to feel ravenous. When a waiter came round with a tray of hot *chorizo* puffs, she seized one with unseemly eagerness and could barely restrain herself from swallowing it whole and grabbing another before the waiter moved on.

'Señora Dryden is a marvellous cook. I wonder what English speciality she is giving us tonight?' said a voice at her elbow.

Cally turned to find a Spaniard of about forty smiling at her. She said, 'I haven't been here before. Does she always serve English specialities?'

'She has on my previous visits. The first time it was steak and kidney pie, and the next time a "hot pot" from the northern part of England. I am Luis Alvarez from Valencia.' He offered his hand.

'Cally Haig from London.'

'You are British?' He looked surprised. 'I thought you might be French. I know our host and hostess have many French friends. How is it that you speak Spanish so well and dress with such panache?'

Amused by his flirtatious flattery, she said, 'I was born in Spain. Are you driving back to Valencia tonight, Señor Alvarez?'

'No, I am invited for breakfast as well as dinner so that I can enjoy Todd Dryden's wines which are always excellent.'

While they were talking there was a gradual shift in the grouping as people moved to make room for the waiter to circulate and their hosts made introductions. Suddenly Cally found herself looking at Nicolás at the same time that he was scanning the room.

Their eyes met and, for a moment, she felt as if everyone else had evaporated, leaving only the two of them. Afterwards, she had no idea what reaction, if any, she had shown. She only knew that Nicolás's gaze rested on her without any sign of recognition and, after a fleeting pause, passed on.

Was it possible that he really hadn't recognised her? Or had she just received a deliberate cut?

Soon after this Leonora rang a bell and, as people stopped talking, announced that dinner was being served in a room downstairs and there was a table plan taped to the door to help everyone find their places.

'I happen to know that I am to have the pleasure of sitting next to you,' said Luis Alvarez. 'Shall we go down?'

He finished the wine in his glass and, when Cally had done the same, took both glasses and, when they reached the doorway, put them on a table with other discarded glasses.

Nicolás watched them leave the room and wondered who the man was.

Since his abrupt departure from the *casa rural*, he had tried not to think about Cally. But although he had had many other things on his mind, images of her kept intruding: her coolness when he arrived, her gradual warming towards him, her passionate response to his kiss, her angry, accusing face when she told him to leave.

He had not expected her to be here tonight and, for an instant, hadn't recognised the glamorous creature on the far side of the room who had looked through him for a few seconds before turning to smile at her visibly captivated companion.

Who would not be captivated by that luscious mouth and the curves enticingly revealed by the black lace top? thought Nicolás, while listening with apparent interest to a commentary on Spanish politics, a subject high on his list of tedious party topics.

He had known that Cally had style, in an understated way, but that she was capable of looking the acme of sophisticated allure was a revelation.

His desire to possess her revived. Not that it had been

diminished by her fury the last time they met. He had merely put it on hold while organising the lease of La Higuera and attending to matters to do with his latest business venture.

'We are at the Red Table,' said Luis, as he and Cally reached the bottom of the staircase. 'I was given a preview. It's the second table on the right.'

Instead of joining the line-up to see the table plan, he steered her around it and into the large dining room where four round tables were each set with six places. Each table had a different colour scheme, the others being yellow, green and white.

At all the tables, place cards indicated where guests were to sit. Luis was on Cally's right. To her dismay, she saw that Nicolás was going to be on her left. Had she been the firstcomer at the table, she would quickly have switched his card with that of the third man at the table. But she couldn't do that with Luis watching...or could she?

Acting on a powerful desire not to be elbow-to-elbow with Nicolás for the next couple of hours, she whipped his place card out of its antique silver holder and made the changeover.

Seeing Luis raising his eyebrows and looking intrigued, she said, 'I particularly want to sit next to Señor Bermejo. I've wanted to meet him for ages.'

'Does that mean you are going to cold-shoulder me?' he asked teasingly.

'Of course not. But there will be times when you'll want to talk to your other neighbour,' she said, with a gesture at the place on his right.

'The others may be some minutes. Let's sit down and chat.' He did not draw out her chair before his own as Nicolás would have done, she noticed. 'I'm an art dealer.

What are you? Let me guess…something to do with the fashion world?'

'I've been in publishing in London for the past five years.'

'The UK has some excellent art publishers.' He named three. 'You are not with any of them, are you?'

Cally shook her head. 'Biographies and memoirs are my field.'

When he asked her the name of her publisher, to avoid going into details that couldn't be of any interest to him and would be painful to her, she simply gave him the name of Edmund & Burke.

At this point they were joined by Señor Bermejo, a man in his late fifties accompanied by his wife who gave Cally's outfit the disapproving glance of someone who saw younger women as a threat to her marital security. Perhaps her husband was rich, thought Cally. There was certainly no other reason why anyone should make eyes at him. She was surprised to find such a dull-looking pair on the Drydens' guest list.

The next person to arrive was the woman placed next to Luis. She looked more lively than the Bermejos. She introduced herself as Gabriela, a physiotherapist who painted in her spare time.

The last to find his way to the table was Nicolás. As he bowed to the women on either side of him, Luis murmured in Cally's ear, 'Now if you had wanted *him* beside you I could have understood it.' In a louder voice, looking at the younger man, he said, 'Welcome to our group, *señor*. You find yourself with a physiotherapist—' with a gesture at Gabriela '—a publisher from London—' another gesture to his left '—and I am an art dealer. We have yet to learn how Señor Bermejo occupies himself.'

'I am Señor Dryden's lawyer.' the older man announced importantly.

'We are honoured, sir,' Luis said gravely. 'And you?' looking enquiringly at Nicolás.

Cally had fixed her gaze on the flowers in the centre of the table, but when she heard him reply, 'I work for a service provider,' she couldn't stop herself giving him a startled look. She had expected him to say either that he was in property or the hotel industry.

'Is that something to do with the Internet?' the lawyer asked, frowning.

'It's the means by which Internet users gain access to the Net,' said Nicolás. 'Around the world there are many service providers. But we like to think that we are the best in Spain. The other Spanish SPs wouldn't agree of course,' he added smiling.

'If you ask me, it's high time you people were brought under proper control,' Señor Bermejo said brusquely. 'Without adequate regulation...' He launched on a long tirade against an environment that, in his view, encouraged every kind of criminality.

This continued through the service of the first course and while everyone's glass was filled with a white wine to accompany the poached salmon salad.

'So what have you to say to that?' the lawyer demanded, his appetite finally stemming his oratory.

'Not a great deal,' Nicolás said, his tone mild. 'I personally believe the Net is the world's best hope for understanding and tolerance...but not if politicians and the legal profession take control of it.'

'I agree,' Gabriela said warmly. 'I think it's a wonderful medium for creativity.'

'It's certainly an invaluable means of advertising,' said Luis.

'What do you think, *señorita*?' Nicolás asked, looking at Cally. 'Your publishing house has a website, I imagine?'

'Of course…it's a very important tool for promoting our authors' books,' she agreed.

The discussion continued throughout the first course, with the lawyer refusing to be influenced by the others' opinions and his wife supporting him on a subject of which she had even less knowledge than he.

'Time for a change of topic, don't you think?' Luis murmured to Cally.

Watching the dealer whisper something in her ear, Nicolás thought he looked as glib as a used car salesman. The strength of his antipathy towards a man he didn't know surprised him.

He was also surprised by the discovery that Cally was a publisher, though that was an elastic term that might mean anything from editor to publicist to marketing person. But the fact that she had a career and was not, as he had thought, a dogsbody for her parents, was good news. But why hadn't she told him earlier? What reason could she have had for keeping it quiet? Normally, people with interesting jobs talked about them, and their discussions about books had given her many cues to reveal that she was involved in their production.

At close quarters—though he would have preferred to be sitting in the pompous ass lawyer's chair—she was even more ravishing than from across the room upstairs. He would enjoy finding out how that black lacy thing unfastened…and she would enjoy it too, if only they were on terms that allowed him to ask her back to La Higuera for coffee after the party was over.

Though, in his teens, he had heard other guys thinking out loud what they would like to do to alluring but out-of-reach girls, it had never been his own habit to share such daydreams, or indeed to imagine those scenarios. To find himself doing it now was disconcerting. But from the first time he saw her, Cally had exerted a strange pull on him. He felt sure it would eventually wear off and the best way to make it do that was to spend time in bed with her. But at the moment she despised him, and not without reason, given that he hadn't explained that the rumour about the hotel was untrue.

With hindsight, he ought to have done that. But he had been annoyed that she hadn't liked him enough to give him the benefit of the doubt.

If he had known then that she was a publisher, he probably would have explained. But thinking, at the time, that she didn't have the backbone to make an independent life for herself, he had felt that her ultimatum was probably all for the best.

She hadn't trusted him, and he hadn't trusted her.

The question he had to address now was whether to pursue her. At the moment, even though he wasn't looking at her, merely being within a couple of metres of her threw his judgment out of kilter.

Appearing to be listening attentively to a conversation between the women on either side of him, Nicolás switched off the private part of his mind and tuned in to what they were saying.

It wasn't until the main course was being served that Cally was sufficiently adjusted to the shock of sitting opposite Nicolás to be able to appreciate how much attention to detail had been given to the arrangement of this and the neighbouring tables.

Everything on it from the crimson-bordered side plates to the silver pepper and salt containers, a pair for each place, was unusual and beautiful. Either Leonora Dryden had inherited a treasure trove, or she had been a life-long collector of glasses, china and knives, forks and spoons.

'Cooking for twenty-four people would terrify me,' said Gabriela. 'Leonora enjoys it. She has incredible energy.'

'Creative people are usually creative in more than one direction,' said Luis. He looked at the food on his plate. 'This dish with pork, prunes and apples, from which part of England does it come?' he asked Cally.

'I'm afraid I don't know,' she said. 'I know more about Spanish food than English cooking.'

'Don't you take your authors out to lunch at London's best restaurants?' Nicolás asked her.

'Usually only the mega-sellers are wined and dined at the expensive places. The less well-known authors have to make do with more modest hospitality.' She turned to Luis. 'I expect it's the same in the art world, isn't it?'

'Definitely. I don't take artists to restaurants with Michelin stars unless their work is fetching very high prices,' he said, smiling. 'But I should be delighted to take you to one, the next time you feel like a visit to Valencia. When do you return to London?'

'I only arrived today.' To avoid committing herself to a date with him, or saying when she was going back, she turned to the lawyer. 'Do you go to Valencia much, Señor Bermejo?'

'As little as possible. The traffic gets worse every year. Alicante is the same.'

'I was in Alicante recently. I thought it was a delightful city,' said Nicolás. 'But then I live in Madrid, although for the time being I'm based here in Valdecarrasca. Señora Dryden put me in touch with the owner of a house for rent. He is working in Washington and may not come back for some years. I've taken a three-months lease, with the option to extend it if necessary.'

'What brings you to Valdecarrasca?' Luis asked him.

'A business project in this area, but I can't, at this stage, reveal what it is. It is not, as has been rumoured, a hotel,' he said, glancing at Cally with a glint of mockery in his eyes.

She felt her colour rising. 'I'm afraid you will find it very quiet and dull compared with the excitements of Madrid.'

'Do you find it dull compared with London?'

'I've never been here for three months. I'm usually only here for a week or two weeks.'

To avoid further questions, she turned to Luis. 'Were you born in Valencia? Have you always lived there?'

'I grew up in Sagunto, a little north of Valencia. In my twenties I worked in Paris and Amsterdam. All young people should have a spell of living abroad, don't you think?'—addressing the question to the table as a whole.

This prompted the lawyer to launch another lecture on the bad habits introduced by flighty female tourists and obstreperous foreign youths. Cally and Gabriela exchanged silent looks, though, privately, Cally preferred being bored by Bermejo to being baited by Nicolás.

She didn't understand why, if his project wasn't a hotel, he hadn't said so when she confronted him. Perhaps it was something worse than a hotel. A rowdy disco, a casino. Either would be a blight on the valley.

After the main course had been cleared and before the pudding was served, Todd Dryden rose and, clinking a spoon against his glass to catch people's attention, asked for all the men present to change places with the men on their left.

'We always do this at our parties. It gives all the ladies at your table the chance to enjoy sitting next to you,' he explained. 'And, in a moment, Leonora and I will also change places with two of our guests.'

The changeover brought Nicolás to Cally's right side, with Luis now on her left. A few minutes later their host asked his lawyer if he would mind moving to the yellow table so that Todd Dryden could sit between Señora Bermejo and Gabriela.

Dryden was much better company than the lawyer and even his wife became less po-faced sitting beside the good-humoured American.

The pudding was a brandied fig tart with home-made apricot ice cream. 'This is one of my wife's specialities,' he told them. 'You can see how difficult it is for me to keep my weight down, married to such a superb cook. I hope you'll like the dessert wine I've chosen to go with it.'

As the others started talking about wine, Nicolás turned to Cally. 'Why didn't you tell me you were in publishing?'

'When I'm in Spain, on holiday, I tend not to think about my working life.'

'You were working a lot of the time I was staying with you,' he said dryly. 'I had the impression you lived in Valdecarrasca.'

'Did you? I'm surprised you didn't realise my parents' business couldn't support a third person, even if someone of my age would be content to stay in such a small place. Perhaps you didn't give it a great deal of thought,' she said coolly, her tone a hair's breadth from hostility.

This was the closest she had been to him since the night they had sat on the sofa and he had kissed her. She was acutely conscious of the athletic body inside the well-cut suit and the broad shoulder close to hers. She remembered the feel of his mouth on hers when all she wanted to think about was the taste of the preserved figs.

'What field of publishing are you in?' he asked.

She had no alternative but tell a white lie. 'I'm a non-fiction editor with Edmund & Burke. You've probably never heard of them. They're not one of the big, well-known imprints.'

'Big isn't necessarily best. Some of the smallest publishers produce the most distinguished books. How did you get into publishing?'

This was not a subject she wanted to discuss with him, but as she could think of no way to avoid the question, she said, 'I did a postgraduate course in publishing that included a work experience placement with Edmund & Burke. At the end of the course they took me on as an assistant in the editorial department.'

'And you've been with them ever since?'

She nodded. 'How did you get into service provision?'

'I was a teenage computer freak. I went to college in the US—I have relations there—and afterwards I spent some time in Silicon Valley. It struck me that service provision was the backbone of the whole show. People I knew in Spain had the same idea and we set up our company when there wasn't as much competition as there is now. We've managed to hold the top place in the efficiency league table of Spanish providers. Some people will always go for the freebie services, but those who need total reliability come to us.'

'I see,' she said politely. What she saw above all was that Nicolás had probably amassed the kind of fortune that, among her father's generation, was not achieved until the late forties or fifties and, for most people, never. But today there were men in their twenties and thirties who were millionaires because they had seen the potential of the new medium and clever ways to exploit it.

To her relief, Luis claimed her attention by asking which part of London she lived in.

'In Chelsea. It used to be the artists' part of the city. There are still a lot of houses with studios with tall windows giving a north light.'

'But now that district is fashionable and expensive,' he said. 'Do you have a house or an apartment?'

'Neither. I have a small bedsitter in a house owned by

someone else.' But maybe not for much longer was her unspoken afterthought.

'It's better to live in the heart of a city than on its out-skirts,' said Luis. 'I am fortunate in having an apartment in the old part of Valencia.' He leaned forward slightly to speak to Nicolás. 'Do you live in central Madrid?'

'Yes,' said Nicolás, but he did not elaborate.

Cally had an intuition that he lived in some exclusive area that only the very rich could inhabit. Yet he did not adver-tise his prosperity as Luis did with his Rolex watch, gold bracelet and rather too large gold signet ring. Nicolás wore an inconspicuous steel watch and his long brown fingers were ringless. Luis's nails looked manicured, but Nicolás's, though clean and short, did not look as if they had ever received professional attention.

When the pudding plates had been removed, coffee was served at the table, with dishes of irresistible hand-made chocolates.

To Cally's relief, for most of the time they were drinking coffee Mr Dryden held their attention with several amusing anecdotes relating to his early days in Spain. This meant that she didn't have to sit braced for Nicolás's next question. But even when they both joined in the laughter, his deep low laugh sent a shiver through her. Even his speaking voice had a timbre to which, unwillingly, she responded, espe-cially when he was speaking his own language with its roll-ing 'r's and the lisped 'c's that, so she had read, originated when a Spanish king had a lisp which, to flatter him, was copied by his courtiers.

Presently, the people at Leonora's table rose and left the room.

'Let's go back upstairs, shall we?' said her husband. 'If you ladies want to repair your lipstick, you can use my wife's bedroom. Go to the top of the stairs and turn right.'

Cally wondered if he slept in a separate room. But when

she and Gabriela joined their hostess and other women, the size of the bed and the books piled on both bedside tables suggested that 'my wife's bedroom' was a figure of speech. Certainly the Drydens gave the impression of enjoying a much warmer relationship than her parents.

When an opportunity arose to have a word with her hostess, she said, 'Mrs Dryden, I hope you won't mind if I slip away rather early by Spanish standards. I was up before six this morning. It's a lovely party, but I may start flagging by midnight.'

'My dear, of course you may leave whenever you like,' Leonora said warmly. 'It was angelic of you to come.' Lowering her voice and speaking English, she said, 'I love our Spanish friends dearly but they are incorrigible night owls and can party till all hours. Todd and I will be washed out tomorrow. We could dance till dawn once, but not now.'

Then, reverting to Spanish, she added, 'Would you like me to ask Nicolás Llorca to walk you home? I'm sure he would be delighted.'

'Oh, no…please don't!' Realising her reply had sounded too emphatic, Cally said, 'It's no distance and no one unpleasant lurks in our streets, thank goodness.'

Leonora gave her a quizzical look. 'No, the village is blessedly safe,' she agreed, 'but being walked home by a personable man is always rather a pleasant experience, don't you think? Or are you less impressed by him than I am?'

'He seems very nice,' Cally said politely. 'But I really don't need an escort, thank you. Is that a portrait of your husband?'—looking at a painting on the wall near her hostess's dressing table.

'Yes, that was Todd when he was twenty-five. It was my first attempt at a portrait and doesn't really do him justice. At that age he was spectacularly handsome, and—in my eyes—still is. Ah, I see the bathroom is free. Do you want to use it. No? Then I shall. Excuse me.'

Before leaving the bedroom, Cally saw that her shawl had been laid on the bed with the other wraps. About half an hour later, after making a discreet exit from the drawing room, she retrieved it and went downstairs and out of the house.

Walking home by empty lamp-lit streets, she realised that now, because of Nicolás's presence in it, Valdecarrasca was no longer a haven from the stresses of London. Here there were other stresses that in some ways were harder to deal with than the uncertainties afflicting her career.

The following day, soon after the Haigs had breakfasted, the doorbell jangled. As her parents were upstairs, changing out of their dressing gowns—which many people in the village wore until late in the morning—to go for a dental check-up, Cally answered it.

For a moment she wondered if the caller could be Nicolás. Local people usually opened the door and shouted to make their presence known. In earlier years, doors had been left unlocked even when people were out. Nowadays most of the village housewives locked up when they went to the shops.

Wishing she had put on lipstick, Cally opened the door and, pierced by mingled relief and disappointment, found Luis standing outside.

'Good morning. I wanted to have a word with you before leaving,' he said.

'Good morning. Come in. I'm surprised you recognised me in my everyday mode,' she said, smiling.

'You look just as charming out of party mode,' he assured her.

Cally laughed. 'Can I offer you a cup of coffee?'

'No, thanks. I've just finished breakfast. What an inter-esting old house'—looking up at the olive wood beams and ancient stone arches. 'You must give me a copy of your brochure. I might be able to steer some clients in your direction.'

'Thank you. Here it is.' She handed him a copy of the leaflet she had designed and had printed. 'Shall we sit down?'—indicating the comfortable armchairs arranged round a table with neat stacks of magazines on it.

'As I don't have to rush back to Valencia, I was wondering if you were free to have lunch with me today…somewhere local,' he said.

'Thank you, but my parents are taking advantage of my being here to have a day out and I need to hold the fort.'

'I understand.' He gave her a thoughtful look. 'In fact I think I understand more than I did last night. When you switched the place cards, it was not because you wanted to meet that buffoon Bermejo, but because you did *not* want to sit next to Nicolás Llorca. Am I right?'

'What makes you think that?'

'There was a tension between the two of you that was obvious to me if not to the others. He is clearly attracted, but it appears not to be mutual. Rather surprising, considering that most women would give him ten out of ten.'

'You have a very active imagination. Perhaps you've missed your vocation and should be writing fiction,' she answered lightly.

When he didn't respond, she added, 'Have you considered that I might be immune to Señor Llorca's charms because I already have a partner in London?'

'If you had, he would be on holiday with you. No sane man would allow you out of his sight.'

Cally burst out laughing. 'I suppose the wealthy art-lovers who patronise your gallery lap up outrageous flattery. You don't really expect me to swallow it, do you?'

He leaned forward. 'I mean it. I think you're lovely. I wish I were Llorca's age. What is he…thirty?'

'Thirty-four according to his identity card. He stayed here for a few nights.'

'I see…and was that when he blotted his copybook in some way?'

'Since you ask, yes it was.'

'I can guess what happened. You were nice to him and he took it as encouragement to make a heavy pass.'

'No, that wasn't the reason,' she told him firmly. 'I heard a rumour that he was involved in converting a deserted old house across the valley into a hotel. I was angry and told him to leave. You heard him say last night at dinner that his project isn't a hotel, but I think it may be something equally damaging to the atmosphere of the valley. Not that there's anything I can do to stop him, but I don't have to be civil to him…except in other people's houses.'

'I see,' said Luis. 'Why not ask him what his project is? Then, if it's something seriously damaging to the quality of life here, you can lobby the various departments in charge of such matters to have it stopped. I have friends in local government. I may be able to point you in some useful directions. Let me give you my card.' He took a wallet from the inside pocket of his expensive-looking sports coat and produced a high quality business card.

'If there's any way in which I can help…'

'Thank you, you're very kind. But I suspect that Nicolás also has influential contacts,' she said, with a wry expression.

At this point her parents came downstairs. After being introduced, Luis took his leave.

'He's far too old for you,' said her mother, when he had gone. 'Anyway you'd be a fool to marry a Spaniard. I've seen a lot of mixed marriages. They hardly ever work.'

'Mum, he came in to pick up a brochure…not to start a relationship,' Cally said, rolling her eyes.

'He fancies you…anyone can see that,' said Mrs Haig.

'That's just his art dealer's manner. It doesn't mean anything.' Cally looked at her watch. 'You'd better get going.'

She was glad to have the house to herself. Later she went for a walk on a path by the dry, stony bed of a river that, fifty years ago, had carried a flow of water in which children could swim and women could wash clothes. Now the river only ran, briefly, after infrequent spells of heavy rain. Most of the year it was full of wild grasses and bordered by red and pink oleander bushes.

When she got back, Cally went online to pick up emails, hoping there might be some news about jobs. The last email to download had the name Nicolás Llorca alongside the symbol of a closed envelope. The subject of the message was *If you want the facts...*

She opened the message and read... *come for a drink this evening and I'll explain what the project really is. Nicolás.*

Cally read the other emails, wrote answers to two and then returned to his message. She sat staring at the words, debating whether to reply that she would be otherwise occupied this evening but would like to hear about the project another time.

In the end she knew she couldn't contain her curiosity, both about his project and the interior of the house he was renting. She hit the reply button and typed *OK...what time?*

Then she washed a large pear and some grapes and cut a chunk from the loaf fetched from the *panadería* earlier and filled it with the pickled anchovies called *boquerones*. She took her lunch up to the roof terrace and sat in the sun, with Mog looking hopefully up at her, knowing better than to try to jump on her lap but exerting all his considerable feline charm.

'Pickled fish isn't good for pussies,' she told him. But he blinked his eyes and licked his lips so persuasively that eventually she shared one of the anchovies with him.

Later she picked up Nicolás's answer. *Half-past six.*

CHAPTER SIX

ON THE way to La Higuera, Cally dropped a thank-you letter in the mailbox fixed to the wall outside the Drydens' front door. Her grandmother had had old-fashioned notions and, out of respect for her memory, Cally tried to stick to most of Granny's 'rules', among them always writing to thank for hospitality rather than just ringing up.

Although she had put on a slightly modified version of last night's party face, she was casually dressed in jeans and an emerald cotton shirt with a navy sweater slung round her shoulders in case it was cold walking home. Although the days were hot, the temperature dropped sharply after sunset.

Like most Spanish village houses, even the larger ones, the house Nicolás was renting had no space between its façade and the street. Its front step was a step up from the narrow pavement.

Moments after she had pressed the bell-push set in the reveal of the doorway, she heard someone running down a tiled staircase. Then the door was opened and Nicolás loomed above her before he stepped back to allow her to enter. When she was inside, he closed the door and offered his hand.

Cally was used to Spanish manners and would have thought nothing of it had he been anyone else. But shaking hands with Nicolás was different. The pressure of his hard palm against hers, and the grip of his fingers, ignited sensations she would never normally feel during such a commonplace ritual.

'Welcome to my place,' he said, opening an inner door and gesturing for her to precede him. 'It looks a bit unhomely at present because—sensibly—the Fieldings have stored their most treasured possessions in a small house that Mrs Fielding used to live in on the street below this one. But I'll be having some of my belongings brought down to fill the gaps.'

He indicated the chimney-breast where two screws in the plaster were clearly intended to support a large picture.

'I can only offer you wine. White or red?'

'Red, please.'

'You left the Drydens' party early, I gather?'

'I'd had a long day. What time did you leave?'

'Soon after midnight. In the country, I keep country hours.'

He disappeared round the corner of the L-shaped room, leaving Cally in the comfortably furnished living area which opened, through folded-back doors, into a dining section. Out of sight, she presumed, was a kitchen.

There was still enough light for her to see the large court-yard garden at the back of the house. In one corner, its leaves turning yellow, was the fig tree that gave the house its name.

Nicolás returned with a glass of wine in each hand. 'Where would you like to sit?'

'Here will be fine,' said Cally, choosing a tub chair at right angles to a sofa rather than the sofa itself. She had shared a sofa with Nicolás before and did not want to be reminded of that occasion.

He placed one glass on a table beside the chair and took his glass to a table next to a wing chair a couple of metres away.

Then, briefly, he disappeared again, coming back with two pottery dishes, one for her, one for himself.

'I hope you like *maiz frito*. It's all I can offer at the moment. Tomorrow I'll make time to get to a supermarket and stock up properly.'

He did not, she noticed, ask her to recommend one. Perhaps Leonora Dryden had already briefed him on the best places to shop. Or perhaps he was a Twenty-first Century Man who could run his domestic life as efficiently as any woman and only needed a female in the bedroom.

Nicolás sat down and crossed his long legs. He was wearing the chinos she had seen before, with a Madras cotton shirt. His brown tassel loafers were well-polished, worn with cream cotton socks.

'So…here we are again,' he said, 'picking up the threads that were abruptly severed by an erroneous rumour. Do you always believe the worst of people?'

'Not always. The evidence against you seemed pretty conclusive. I gave you a chance to explain yourself. You didn't take it.'

'Perhaps I hoped that already you knew me well enough to feel sure that I wouldn't do anything seriously bad,' he said dryly. 'Or has my suggestion that we go to bed together damned me for ever? That's a little hard to believe in this day and age.'

Aware that her colour had risen, Cally said, 'If it had damned you for ever, I wouldn't be here, would I?' Suddenly aware that this remark was open to misinterpretation, she hurried on, 'And the reason I'm here is to hear what your project is.'

He drank some wine and replaced the glass on the table at his elbow. 'Have you ever heard of West Dean College?'

'It's a craft centre somewhere in the south of England, isn't it?'

'That's right. One of my English cousins is an *aficionada*…she's enrolled for pretty well every course they run. Picture framing…gilding…antique restoration. You name it, she's done it. It's not only popular with the British, but with Americans too, and the reason for that is partly because West Dean is a beautiful old house with fine gardens and a large estate for visitors to explore. According to my cousin, it's a place that refreshes the soul as well as teaching various forms of craftsmanship.'

'Is that what you're planning to set up here...a crafts centre?'

'A centre, but not a crafts centre. The house across the valley isn't comparable with West Dean. It's smaller, it has no estate, and there is no enlightened benefactor like Edward James, who owned West Dean, to bequeath his fortune to fund it. The only money I have is what I have made. At this stage of my life, I don't plan to give it away. Perhaps in fifty years' time...' His wide shoulders moved in a shrug.

'So what sort of centre are you planning?'

'A spin-off from my present interests.'

'Last night you said you worked for a service provider.' She wasn't getting his drift. There seemed no possible link between the high tech stuff he was involved with and a valley in the backwoods of rural Spain where even broadband—continuous and rapid access to the Net—was a distant dream.

'I do. I'm the CEO so I work harder than anyone,' he said, smiling.

As always, his smile did disturbing things to her equilibrium. 'So how come you can take time off to stay here?' she asked, rather crisply.

'Distance is dead,' said Nicolás. 'I'm in constant contact with my colleagues wherever I am. You're not in touch with your office because you're on leave. But you could be, if you wanted. When video-conferencing facilities have been brought to perfection, and every business has them, people like you will be able to work wherever you please.'

Cally was unconvinced, but she didn't say so. She used email but that was the limit of her technological expertise. It wasn't a subject she could discuss with authority.

Nicolás rose and fetched the packet containing the fried

maize grains from the kitchen. When he would have topped up her dish, Cally said, 'No more for me, thanks.'

'Not nice, or too high cal?'

'Very nice…but I'm not much of a nibbler.'

'I am.' He tipped a small cascade into his dish. 'That's why I run in the morning…to counterbalance the sins of the night before.'

'Whatever sins of gluttony you're committing, they haven't started to show yet.' Most of the men of his age she encountered in London were starting to get jowly and paunchy.

'That's the luck of the genes. I come from a long line of giraffe-shaped people.'

'Giraffes don't have broad shoulders.' She regretted the comment the instant it was spoken. 'Tell me more about this centre you're planning.'

His dark eyes mocked her. 'Yes, it's safer to stick to the point. If we wander off it, who knows where we might fetch up?'

Cally was on the point of telling him that she wasn't going to tolerate sexy looks or ambiguous remarks, but she changed her mind and said nothing.

To her relief, the teasing glint was replaced by a serious expression. 'I want to establish a centre of excellence in the field of website design. At the moment anyone with a computer can set themselves up as a designer and the public has no way of telling if they really know what they're doing or are learning as they go along.'

For the next fifteen minutes, he presented his plan to her, speaking with a passionate enthusiasm that made it hard to be sceptical about the practicality of locating the enterprise in such an unlikely setting.

Listening, she realised that here was someone who, under an insouciant manner, was intensely serious. She had heard this tone of voice before from authors expounding a theme for a book.

He sat back and drank some wine. 'You think I'm crazy, I expect. But at least it isn't going to wreck your parents' business. It might even do it some good if we have to use outside accommodation.'

'I don't think you're crazy. I think it's a bit of a gamble.'

'All brilliant ideas are gambles at the beginning. It won't be a huge money-spinner. But it will be a prestige-winner...if I can pull it off.'

He sprang up to go to the kitchen, coming back with the bottle of wine to top up their glasses. In the few moments before he rejoined her, it struck Cally that the way he had sprung from the chair in one elastic movement was characteristic of his whole nature. He was a man of action, a natural innovator and pioneer. Time spent with him would never be dull, she thought. For the woman he married—if he married—life would be an ongoing adventure. It would never deteriorate into a boring routine the way most marriages seemed to.

'Tomorrow, if you like I'll take you over there and show you the house,' he said. 'It needs one helluva lot of doing up, but it has huge potential.'

'How did you find out there was an old empty house there? Did a property agent send you the details?'

'It's my house. It always has been. It was left to me by a great-aunt who had sole ownership. She died when I was a baby, and the place has been falling to pieces ever since and probably long before that. It hasn't been lived in since before our civil war.'

It struck Cally that anyone who had owned a large house in Spain before 1936, when the majority of Spaniards lived in extreme poverty, would have had to be rich. She remembered the woman who had spread the hotel rumour had said that the only person who remembered its owners was old Señora Martinez who had worked there as a maid.

Tomorrow, thought Cally, I'll go and talk to her. She may know things about the place that even Nicolás doesn't know.

'I'd like to see it,' she said. 'But I think you'll have to allow a lot of time for the renovations. This is a far cry from Madrid. Builders around here aren't famous for their speed. There are usually endless delays. There's a new house at the edge of the village which the *alcalde*'s brother is having built for his son. Last time I was here I asked him when it would be finished and he raised his eyes to Heaven and said, *"Dios sabe!"*'

Nicolás laughed. 'I'm prepared for that. But I've got a first-rate architect in charge and he only uses the most reliable builders, not the cowboys. However enough of my plans. I want to hear more about your work. I have a friend who's in publishing in Madrid. He often complains about the British and American resistance to translations of the best books being published in mainland Europe.'

Before she could comment, he added, 'Before we get onto that, will you stay and share a pizza with me? If you say yes, you won't, I promise you, be laying yourself open to an unwelcome follow-up.' He gave her another of those devastating smiles. 'If I had anything like that in mind, I'd have laid on some *cava* and caviare, not something as prosaic as a pizza.'

Despite this assurance, Cally wasn't sure that it was a good idea to resume friendly relations. On the other hand, if she went home, it was likely to be a dull evening, with her father sloping off to watch football as soon as supper was over, and her mother in one of her complaining moods.

'OK, I'll stay,' she agreed.

'Come through to the kitchen. We can talk while I'm throwing a salad together and tarting up the pizza.'

He ushered her round the corner where the unseen part

of the large room proved, as she had thought, to be a well-equipped kitchen which combined every modern convenience with a homeliness provided by the wood-faced cupboards and the marble work-tops usually found in Spanish kitchens. But here, instead of the usual and rather cheerless pale grey marble, the surfaces were rose-coloured veined with brown.

Nicolás turned one of the dining chairs to face the working end of the kitchen. While she sat down, he moved to the other side of the work-top that separated the two areas and started preparing their meal with a casual efficiency that surprised her.

Every time she thought she had him sussed, he revealed a new and unexpected aspect of his character.

'We were going to discuss translations,' he reminded her. 'Does your firm publish any?'

It was an opportunity to tell him that she wasn't working for E&B any more, but she didn't feel ready to share her private anxiety with him. They had shared the intimacy of a passionate embrace. They had also come close to enmity, at least on her side. They were not, and might never be, close friends.

'Not many…hardly any in fact. I was very keen to publish the memoirs of a Spanish Grandee who has had a fascinating life. But I couldn't sell the idea to our marketing people.'

'Which of our Grandees was that?' Nicolás asked. When she told him, he said, 'He's a fabulous guy. I've met him. He's been a bestseller in Spain. How insular of your people not to be willing to give English readers a chance to get to know him. But of course both the Brits and the Americans do tend to be inward-looking nations…and, with some exceptions such as yourself, hopeless linguists.'

'You were going to explain to me why you speak such flawless English. It can't be because of your time in the

US,' she said. 'You speak English-English, not American-English.'

It seemed to her that, for a moment, he looked slightly embarrassed. But perhaps she imagined it, because then he said, 'My mother wasn't able to spend much time with me when I was small. I was in the charge of an elderly Englishwoman who had lived in Spain for a long time but never acquired more than rudimentary Spanish. So we spoke English most of the time.'

Cally remembered reading somewhere that all the great sherry and port dynasties, in southern Spain and Portugal, had employed English nannies to look after their children. She wondered if Nicolás's 'elderly Englishwoman' could have been an early graduate from the famous Norland College of Nursing which had supplied nannies to wealthy people from all over the world.

It would tie in with her earlier supposition that the great-aunt from whom he had inherited the house across the valley must have been rich.

'Since then, of course,' he went on, 'I've spent time in America and England. Has your Spanish been of use to you in your job?'

'Not really.'

'I wonder if the Fieldings have any of your firm's books. Have a look at the bookshelves through there—' with a nod in the direction of the area where they had been sitting. 'You might find something written by one of your authors.'

Cally did as he suggested, but although the owners of the house had a catholic selection of books from all the major UK and US publishing houses, there was nothing with E&B's colophon on the spine.

By the time she returned to the kitchen to report this, Nicolás seemed to have finished his preparations.

'Tonight's supper will be an anticlimax after the feast Leonora gave us last night,' he said. 'I like that couple.

Neither of them has any hang-ups, which makes a change in the stressed-out worlds we live in.'

'You don't seem to suffer from stress.'

'I don't have a mortgage and school fees and keeping up with the Joneses to worry about,' he said, refilling their glasses. 'I'm only responsible for myself...which makes life a whole lot easier. How is your stress level?'

If you only knew! thought Cally.

'Pretty good,' she said cheerfully. 'I don't have a mortgage hanging over me. I pay rent to a friend for a share of her house. She has the mortgage problem, but as it's a lovely house in a highly desirable part of London by the time she retires she's going to be able to buy a mansion in the country if she wants one.'

'Yes, long term, property is usually a pretty good bet,' he agreed. 'Although I notice that several small country houses between here and the coast had their value kiboshed when the *autopista* was built a few metres from their boundaries. That round-the-clock drone of traffic is not part of most people's dream of a life in the sun.'

As she murmured agreement, he added, 'But I think your parents' situation worries you, doesn't it? Do they own the *casa rural* or are they still paying for it?'

'They own it, but they don't have any other income to fall back on if the business declines, so, yes, I do worry about them. Do your parents live in Madrid or the country?'

'They're divorced. My mother lives in Madrid. My father works overseas. My sisters are scattered. We're not a close family. But I have the impression that, although you're a dutiful daughter—perhaps too dutiful for your own good—yours is also what the shrinks like to call a dysfunctional family.'

'Not dysfunctional,' she said, a little indignantly. 'They're not ideally matched, but how many people are?'

'Very few,' he said dryly. 'Which I guess is why our

generation are wary of tying the knot without a trial run first…and a lot of those don't work out.'

'You wouldn't expect them to,' said Cally. 'If people aren't sure at the outset, the chances of it working are minimal.'

'I agree with you there. All the so-called "partnerships" I know are a cop-out on the guy's part. He wants all the benefits of a wife without the responsibility. The women involved must know that, but they choose not to face it, half a loaf being better than no bread. Why do women undervalue themselves? Why don't they say, "No, if you want me, it's all or nothing"? They have this enormous power over men, but they almost never exert it.'

'I suppose it's hard to be strong when you're in love with someone. I haven't been in love, so I wouldn't know.'

But even as Cally said it she knew that it was a lie. She had fallen in love with Nicolás. Exactly when, she wasn't sure, but before she had sent him packing. That was why it had made her so angry to discover what, then, had seemed like his treachery.

His black eyebrows rose. 'You've never been in love. How old are you?'

'Twenty-seven. Well, I've been through calf love,' she conceded. 'But that doesn't really count. Have you ever been in love…seriously in love?'

He shook his head. 'Not so far. I like women. I enjoy their company. But to commit to one person for the rest of one's life is a pretty scary undertaking. When you meet people like Todd and Leonora, who obviously care for each other as much now as when they first got together, it looks a great way to live. But couples like them aren't thick on the ground.'

'I wonder why it has worked for them?' Cally said thoughtfully.

'From what I was told about them by other people at the

party, I should say it's because they've given each other a lot of back-up.'

'What do you mean?'

'She followed him round the world when he was in the oil business, and he's always encouraged her to paint and helped finance her flair for restoring old properties which she used to do a lot when they first settled in Spain. I'm going to consult her about my place. Are you ready to eat?'

'Whenever you are. Can I do anything to help?'

'You can put these on the table.' He handed her two place-mats and a handful of cutlery.

When she had arranged them, Cally debated asking if she should draw the long curtains at the two tall living room windows and the single window in the dining area. The back door was also glazed but, as was often seen in Spain, had a hinged wooden shutter on the inside. She decided not to suggest drawing the curtains but to leave it to him to close them if he wished.

In the light of that shattering moment of self-discovery— when her claim never to have been in love had revealed to her that she was in love—and now that her curiosity about his project had been satisfied, it would have been more sensible to have declined his invitation to stay. After tonight, she would have to be strong-minded and resist any more friendly overtures.

He had made it clear that he wasn't in the market for any serious relationship, and she wasn't in the market for an affair, however enjoyable it might be at the beginning.

Anyway, as he had said himself, women's power over men lay in resistance not surrender. As long as she kept him at arm's length, she would be a challenge to him. Once she succumbed, she would join the list of women he had enjoyed and discarded. Because clearly he hadn't spent his twenties in monastic celibacy. As someone at E&B had said of another attractive man, 'If the girls he's laid were laid end to end, they'd stretch from London to Birmingham.'

Cally didn't want to think about how far a line of Nicolás's past amours might stretch. But she knew she was not going to join the line. The only kind of relationship she wanted was one like the Drydens had. Failing that, she would rather live life on her own.

They had finished eating and were having coffee in the living room when he suggested they watched the CNN news. Cally seldom watched TV in London and almost never in Spain.

When the bulletin was over, she rose. 'I must go now. Thank you for supper.'

He made no attempt to persuade her to stay, but insisted on walking her home.

Outside the *casa rural* she offered her hand. 'Thank you again for the meal.'

'My pleasure.' He lifted her hand and brushed her knuckles, repeating the gesture she had witnessed the night before when he greeted Leonora Dryden.

'Goodnight.' He turned and walked back up the street, the way they had come.

When Nicolás returned to La Higuera, it seemed to him that a faint fragrance of her scent lingered in the air.

He washed the few dishes by hand, thinking how much better it would have been had she stayed the night so that, waking late, they could have had breakfast together.

His bachelor pad in Madrid had a different atmosphere. This house was designed for two people. It made him conscious of his one-ness. He had always protected his privacy, enjoyed his own company. But tonight he was suddenly aware that solitude, like everything else, had its downside: it was a near neighbour of loneliness.

The living room was not the only room with books. They

were everywhere; in the hall, on the landing, in all the bedrooms. Before going to bed, he trawled the shelves looking for the Edmund & Burke colophon. He found three of their titles and put them on the bedside table to look at later. Then he booted up his laptop, checked his emails and, having dealt with them, did a search for the publisher's website. He spent some time there, making notes to discuss with Cally the next time he saw her.

In bed he examined the three books, not intending to read them, but interested in their presentation. He felt that, generally speaking, British book production was not as good as American. But these books had excellent jackets, decent bindings and were printed on good quality paper without skimped margins.

In one he found a dedication which concluded '…and to Cally Haig, my editor, who made the whole process so much less painful than it might have been. Without her constant encouragement—and occasional, well-deserved raps on the knuckles—it would never have been finished on time. Unquestionably, she is one of the pearls of her profession.'

The tribute had been written by a man who, judging by his photo on the back jacket flap, had a good deal of charisma.

Nicolás wondered if their relationship had been personal as well as professional. Changing his mind, he began to read.

Cally spent a restless night. In several long wakeful periods, she grappled with the catastrophic revelation that her heart was no longer her own but, against her conscious will, had found its way into someone else's keeping. It was an uncomfortable feeling, which was obviously why her mind had tried to deny that it had happened.

Getting up at her usual early hour, despite lack of sleep, she composed a brief thank-you note to be emailed to

Nicolás when she picked up the incoming emails. To her surprise, when they downloaded there was one from him with the subject line *E&B's website*.

She was even more surprised when she opened the message and saw that it was an itemised and highly critical analysis of her previous employer's website. Later, reading a print-out she was surprised yet again by his comment, 'Obviously whoever is in charge of the site is not looking at other publishers' sites and learning from them. A good way to attract visitors is to have messageboards where readers can discuss books they have/have not enjoyed. See, for example the messageboards at *www.eharlequin.com.*'

Cally knew that Harlequin was arguably the world's best-known romance publisher, but she wouldn't have expected him to know it. How and when had he acquired that esoteric bit of knowledge? Had one of his girlfriends been a romance reader? Next time they met she would ask him.

And next time she would also have to admit that she wasn't with E&B any more. However humiliating it might be to explain that she had been sacked, it was time to be upfront with him. If she went on deceiving him and somehow he found out, that would be even more damaging to his opinion of her.

She wished his opinion was a matter of indifference to her. But, if she were honest, suddenly it mattered a lot.

CHAPTER SEVEN

AT THE end of November, Valdecarrasca was the scene of a small but popular arts and crafts fair that attracted people of all nationalities. For a couple of weeks beforehand, banners proclaiming a *Feria de Artesanía* hung across the main street to catch the eye of motorists passing through.

The fair took place in the *plaza mayor* where about thirty stalls were crowded together, and the local bars sold more drinks and coffees in two days than they did in a month of normal business. Every available street parking space in the village was occupied and the visitors' cars lined the roads outside it and some of the lanes through the vineyards.

The fair continued after dark and this year there were some Christmas-style illuminations suspended above the square to show that, despite its small population, Valdecarrasca was keeping up with the times.

A similar *feria* took place in the spring. A few years earlier, Cally had been home for Easter and bought several presents at the fair, including one for herself, a hand-printed silk scarf in the sea-water colours she loved. This time she hoped to find gifts for Olivia, Deborah and other friends in the UK.

She had her first look round the stalls at mid-morning on the Saturday. At the previous fair, so her parents had told her, there had been complaints that professional street vendors were taking over an event intended to be a showcase for local artists and craftsmen. But this time the balance was in their favour though, to Cally's disappointment, the woman from whom she had bought her beautiful scarf was not there.

She was looking at hair ornaments made from old silver forks with their tines fashioned into curls and squiggles when there was one of the traffic snarl-ups that punctuated *feria* days. The stall where she was standing was close to the road when the usual barrage of hooting broke out.

She heard a British voice say, 'Cor...I wouldn't mind having that!'

Another voice replied, 'You'd need to win the lottery to buy it...and to pay for the petrol. A car like that doesn't go far on a tankful.'

Looking round, Cally saw that the car they were discussing was a sleek metallic silver drophead coupé with its roof down. The man at the wheel was the only one in the line-up who wasn't using his horn or shouting advice to the village policeman who was trying to sort out the bottleneck. He looked both relaxed and amused.

The man at the wheel was Nicolás.

Cally moved to the railing which separated the central part of the *plaza* from the roadway for a closer look. Not being much interested in cars, she had no idea what make or model it was. But, as the two men had said, it was obviously very expensive. It was just as well that La Higuera had a garage, she thought. Street-parking a car like that would be asking for trouble, not only in the way of accidental damage but also malicious damage by the sort of people who resented anyone having something they could never afford themselves. Not that acts of vandalism happened in places like Valdecarrasca on the scale that they did in big cities like London. One of the things she liked about village life was not having to be on one's guard all the time.

Suddenly Nicolás looked up and saw her. The change in his expression from resigned patience to active pleasure sent a shiver of delight through her. Just then the traffic started moving. As he drove past where she was standing, he said,

'Don't go away. I want to talk to you. I'll be with you in a few minutes.'

An old man from the village who spent a lot of his life leaning on the railing, watching the world go by, turned to look at her.

'What did he say to you?' he asked, with the uninhibited curiosity of countrymen of his generation. 'Was it a *piropo*?'

A *piropo*, Cally knew, was an amorous compliment paid by men to passing women, usually something more imaginative and flattering than the sort of remarks shouted by building site workers in England.

She shook her head. 'He's renting a house in the village. He wants to speak to me.'

'Hmph…seems a strange place for a young fellow with a car like that to want to stay.' The old man shook his head in perplexity at the incomprehensible vagaries of human behaviour. Then, peering at her more closely, he added, 'Still you're as pretty a girl as he'll find in any big city. If I were a young man I'd want to talk to you too.'

Cally laughed, '*Gracias, señor.* I'm sure when you were a young man, all the prettiest girls hoped you would talk to them.'

He chuckled. 'Perhaps…it's a long time ago. Enjoy being young while you can. Before you know it, you'll be as old as I am.'

He shuffled away to join another old man, leaving Cally to wait for Nicolás.

It was not long before she saw him entering the *plaza* from its upper end. As the square was now very congested, she went to meet him.

'How about a coffee…if we can find a free table?' he said, when they met by a stall selling hand-made toys.

They were lucky. A party of four well-dressed Germans were about to vacate one of the tables under the pepper tree.

'You stake a claim and I'll go in and get the coffee,' said

Nicolás, who evidently knew that the café did not have table service.

As she waited for him to join her, the loudspeakers around the *plaza* began to relay an old-fashioned love song that she had been hearing at intervals all her life. The singer had been one of Spain's most popular artistes since before Cally was born. When she was small, and her parents were living in the south of Spain, her ambition had been to become a flamenco dancer.

As her feet tapped in time with the music and her eyes followed the ebb and flow of people, Cally knew she would remember this sunlit morning and these moments, waiting for Nicolás, all her life. She had no idea why he wanted to talk to her. It was enough that he did.

This was happiness…fleeting…unjustified…but authentic.

He came back with two cups and saucers, two glasses of wine and two boat-shaped dishes of almonds on a tin tray. Having arranged them on the table, he took the tray back inside and then came and settled his tall frame in the chair beside hers.

'I've been reading *River of Life, Death and Love*. I found it upstairs, the night you had supper with me. It's a marvellous book…with high praise for your input in the foreword. Has the author got another book in the pipeline?'

'Yes, but unfortunately I shan't be editing it, and he may have to move to another publishing house.'

Nicolás raised an eyebrow. 'How come?'

'I'm afraid I've misled you. I was with Edmund & Burke, but I'm not any more. I've been "let go" as they say. I— I didn't mean to deceive you. I just didn't want to talk about it at first.'

'When did it happen?' he asked.

'It was in the air when you were staying with us, but the axe didn't fall until I got back to London. It's one of those corporate reshuffle things that happen more often than they used to. There's really no such thing as job security these days. I imagine it's much the same here, though I don't have many contacts in the Spanish big business world...well, actually, none.'

'I do,' he said. 'Have you thought about looking for an editing job in this country?'

'I've thought about it, but, although my Spanish is OK for everyday purposes, I don't think I could do a good job editing in Spanish. I was educated in England so I know about English literature and English allusions, but I don't have the same sort of grasp of Spanish literature. You have to have an absolutely perfect command of a language to write in it, or to edit it, and translators need a perfect command of two languages to do their job really well.'

Looking thoughtful, Nicolás drank some coffee. 'I take it you've already made efforts to find another job in London?'

'Of course, and I'm keeping a close eye on the job ads on publishers' websites. The trouble is that this isn't the only purge that has happened recently. There are a lot of people in the same boat. If *River* had been a bestseller, Rhys and I could both have relocated fairly easily. But it didn't get the kind of promo that makes a bestseller. Excellent reviews after publication, but not enough hype beforehand.'

'Where is Rhys now?' he asked.

'He's gone to India again, hoping to find another subject for a book. We keep in touch by email. I think one of the most surprising things in *River* is the fact that so many of the villages along the banks of the Ganges have facilities for sending emails.'

'It didn't surprise me as much as it would many people,' said Nicolás. 'When I was working in Silicon Valley in California, I discovered that India has produced an amazing number of guys who are brilliant Net technologists. If they all took their expertise home, India could lead the world in that field...and may yet do so. Tell me more about Rhys. What did he mean by the reference to you rapping his knuckles?'

Cally laughed. 'He has a problem sticking to a routine which is what authors have to do. It's no use waiting for inspiration. They have to work every day, no matter what. Mental exercise is exactly like physical exercise. You have to stick with it, regardless of all distractions.'

'Do you miss him?'

The question perplexed her. 'Miss him? What do you mean?'

'Did you have a personal relationship as well as a working one?'

Cally shook her head. 'What made you think we might have?'

'It happens when people work closely together.'

'Actually we didn't...not in a physical sense. It was almost all done by email.'

'People can fall in love by email,' said Nicolás. 'Being attracted by someone's mind is probably a better basis for a solid relationship than the physical attraction which is the usual starting point.'

'Possibly...but Rhys's emotions were already engaged when he sent the first chapters of the book to me and I commissioned it. He's still in love with the woman who canoed down the Ganges with him. Didn't you get the message that his companion on the trip was the most important person in his life? If not, what did you think the ''love'' in the title referred to?'

'The book's ending seemed to suggest that the love element was a transitory thing, that there was no future for them.'

Cally sighed. 'Unfortunately, I don't think there is. Lucinda enjoyed that adventure with him. But Rhys wants to go on having adventures and she wants a more settled life with babies and friends of her own kind coming to dinner parties. Considering how conventional she is, it's amazing he persuaded her to go at all really.'

'She was in love with him presumably. Women do amazing things for love.'

'But if she loved him, and still does, you'd think she'd put his happiness ahead of her own. Rhys is the kind of man who could never settle to suburbia.'

'You could also argue that, if he loves her, he would put her happiness first. Spending long periods in interesting but uncomfortable and even dangerous places is not how most women want to live.'

Cally finished her coffee before she said, 'I suppose I'm prejudiced in Rhys's favour because he's such a wonderful writer. I think he needs her love and support, and that she's lucky to be loved by such a gifted man. It's interesting that you see the issue from her point of view.'

'I don't see it from her viewpoint so much as from a realistic viewpoint,' said Nicolás. 'It doesn't sound as if they're ideally matched. Maybe he would do better to wait until he finds someone who will love him *and* his lifestyle. I don't think it's a good idea for people to go against their deepest instincts and adjust to someone else's needs. In my observation, that's not a good start for any kind of joint enterprise.' He picked up his glass of wine. *'Salud.'*

'Salud.'

As Cally echoed the toast, a couple approached their table. 'Would you mind if we joined you? It's so crowded today.'

'Not at all,' Nicolás said politely, half rising from his chair as the woman, taking his consent for granted, seated herself on the other side of him.

She was a sixtysomething, trying to pass as a fortysomething. The man with her had strands of hair pasted sideways across his bald patch and everything he was wearing had the designer's name on it.

'We've come over from Calpe,' she said. 'Some friends have lent us their flat. We're from Bootle in Lancashire. Where are you from?'

'I'm from Madrid and my friend is from London,' said Nicolás. 'To order, you have to go inside but, if you like, I'll do the ordering for you. It's a bit of a mad house in there.'

'Would you? That's ever so kind. We don't speak any Spanish. Our friends said we wouldn't need to as long as we stayed in Calpe, but we wanted to explore a bit and someone told us there was a fair on here. My name's Nora and this is Freddie,' said the woman.

To Cally's astonishment, Nicolás told her their first names. Then he went to fetch what the newcomers wanted to drink.

Later, when Freddie asked what they owed him, he said, 'Please…be my guests. At *fiestas* and *ferias* it's the custom to make strangers welcome, particularly when they take the trouble to explore our countryside.' He lifted his glass to them. 'To an enjoyable day for all of us.'

Cally took little part in the conversation that followed. The two visitors had plenty to say for themselves, and Nicolás fed them with questions and appeared to be genuinely interested in their answers.

Eventually, when Cally had finished her wine, he rose and said, 'Will you excuse us? We must finish our tour of the stalls. Goodbye.' He shook hands with them.

As they moved away, Cally heard Nora murmur, 'What a nice fellow.'

She had to agree with Nora. Nicolás had been extremely nice which, considering that the English couple were what Olivia classified as 'people you wouldn't want to be stuck on the trans-Siberian express with', was rather amazing.

'Why were you so nice to them?' she asked, when they were well out of earshot.

'Nice?' he said, looking puzzled. It seemed he had not overheard Nora's comment to Freddie. 'If you were in a pavement café in London and a Spanish couple asked to share your table, wouldn't you be pleasant to them?'

'Of course…but I wouldn't necessarily buy them drinks and encourage them to tell me their life histories.'

He laughed. 'I'm in a good mood today. The sun is shining. There's music. I have a charming companion. In such circumstances, who wouldn't be pleasant to strangers? But I haven't lost all my critical faculties.' He bent his head to say quietly, close to her ear, 'The pictures at the next stall are the most horrible daubs I've seen for a long time.'

'I was thinking the same thing,' said Cally, her ear and the side of her neck tingling in reaction to his intimate undertone.

Further on they came to a stall where, a first glance, there appeared to be two small children gazing intently at something. At second glance they were life-size dolls dressed in baggy trousers and sweaters with caps and hats on their heads. Behind the stall was a row of similar dolls, all standing with their backs to the passersby.

Cally would have liked to see what their fronts were like, but the stall-holder was busy talking to someone.

'What do you think of this silver jewellery?' Nicolás asked, further on.

'It's a bit plain for my taste. But somebody who's into minimalism would love it. Are you looking for Christmas presents for your sisters?' she asked.

'I always give books at Christmas and I usually buy them online to save myself having to wrap them. You probably enjoy gift-wrapping. Most women seem to.'

'Yes, I do. I love choosing paper and ribbons and tags, though they're easier to find in London than here.'

'Will you be here for Christmas?'

'Yes, we're fully booked so there'll be a lot of work to do. Where will you spend Christmas?'

'Possibly on the French side of the Pyrenees. I haven't decided yet. Helping your parents cope with a crowd of oldies doesn't sound like much fun.'

'Oldies can sometimes be more interesting than young people...Mr and Mrs Dryden, for example.'

'Judging by the batch of oldies I met while I was staying with you, the Drydens aren't typical members of the expat community.'

'Not typical—no. But they're not unique. There are other interesting older people living here. Anyway Christmas is no big deal for me. When I was small Three Kings was more important. Now the village people celebrate both and the whole "festive season"—' she wiggled her forefingers '—has become a massive spending spree which, I think, tends to spoil it.'

'I agree,' said Nicolás. 'That's why for the past couple of years I've spent the holiday mountain-walking and avoiding the commercialised rave-up. Probably one will take a different view if and when one has children.'

His last remark surprised her. It was difficult to imagine him in any kind of domestic setting. She felt he belonged in the fast lane with other successful, ambitious, self-sufficient people for whom a wife and a family were not the primary motivations they were for life's also-rans.

She had thought she belonged there too, that her career mattered more than a personal relationship. But having her career put on hold had made her spend more time thinking about her priorities. Even before she knew she had fallen in love, she had been beginning to wonder if she had allowed the failure of her first relationship to weigh too heavily on her.

'Nicolás...what are you doing here?' someone said, in

Spanish, before a man she had never seen before clapped Nicolás on the shoulder.

'Hello, Simón… I didn't expect to see you, although I'd heard you had a place in this area. I was going to look you up later. Cally, this is Simón Mondragón, an old friend of mine. Simón…Cally Haig.' He said the last words in English.

'How do you do, Miss Haig?' The other man offered his hand. Like Nicolás, he was tall and black-haired. Indeed they could have been brothers, Simón being some years older.

'How do you do?' Cally liked him on sight.

'Yes, I have a house at Castell de los Toros,' he said, referring to Nicolás's remark. 'It's been converted into a hostel where children from the poor quarters of our big cities can have a taste of country life. My wife and I come down from time to time to see how the project is going. She heard there was an arts and crafts fair in Valdecarrasca and insisted I bring her…the shops in Madrid having such a poor selection of Christmas gifts,' he added, with a grin.

'Are you accusing me of being a shopaholic, Simón?' asked an attractive woman, emerging from the crush in time to hear this remark. Holding out her hand to Nicolás, and smiling warmly at him, she said, 'The last time you saw me I was in my bridal finery, and now I'm a downtrodden housewife, kept perpetually pregnant by this unregenerate male chauvinist,' giving her husband a mock-reproachful look.

His reaction was to laugh and put an arm round her. 'Not *perpetually* pregnant, my darling.' Looking at Cally, he said, 'We've been married six years and have a four-year-old son. We're hoping the baby who's due to arrive in February will be a daughter. Cassia, this is Cally Haig.'

As the two women shook hands, Nicolás said, 'You mean

you're not sure of its sex? I thought now parents knew what they were getting from quite early on.'

'They can if they have a scan,' said Cassia. 'But as I sailed through my first pregnancy, I'm trying to get through the second with as little medical interference as possible. If you let them, doctors will take over and turn having a baby into a form of illness when it should be as natural as a ewe dropping a lamb on the mountainside…well, perhaps not as easy as that, but not a succession of medical procedures. But, enough of my delicate condition, why don't we go to the bar for a coffee break?'

'The bar is packed. Why not come and have coffee in my garden?' Nicolás suggested. 'It's only a couple of streets away.'

'You're living in this village?' said Simón, looking surprised.

'I'm renting a house that belongs to Cameron Fielding, the TV reporter. You've probably seen him on the box, Cassia.'

She shook her head. 'You forget I've never lived in the UK.' To Cally, she said, 'I sound English but I'm actually a nomad. When Simón swept into my life I was living in the old Moorish part of Granada.'

'You can tell each other your life stories when we get to Nicolás's place,' said her husband.

Half an hour later, relaxing in the peaceful seclusion of La Higuera's courtyard, drinking champagne with the men while Cassia drank chilled orange juice, Cally explained her own background to Simón's wife.

Although by now the fig tree had lost most of its leaves and those that remained kept falling with a rustle on the flagstones, the courtyard did not have the bare look of north-ern European gardens in November. A crimson bougainvillaea was in bloom and a magnificent aeonium was putting out large yellow heads composed of small star-like flowers.

While the women spoke English, the men had reverted to *castellano*. It was clear they had much in common. Presently Cally heard the older man say, 'So you're going to follow my example and adapt your inheritance to a twenty-first century purpose.'

She also caught Nicolás's reply, 'My inheritance is a flea-bite compared with yours,' and wondered what he meant.

Presently, turning to the women, he said, 'I'm going to show Cally my ruin on the other side of the valley. Would you like to come with us? Afterwards we could have lunch at a place I've heard about.'

'I think, if you don't mind, we'll look at your ruin another day,' said Simón. 'Cassia is beginning to look tired. But why not come and dine with us this evening? It's not far…only about half an hour.'

'We'd be delighted. That's all right with you, is it, Cally?' Nicolás asked.

'I'm afraid I can't manage this evening. My parents are going out and someone has to be there in case a visitor arrives. My parents run a *casa rural*,' she explained to the others.

'Couldn't Juanita stand in for you?' Nicolás suggested.

'Not tonight, I'm afraid.'

She hoped he would not ask why. To her relief, he didn't.

'Then I'll come on my own,' said Nicolás. 'There are one or two legal complexities you have probably dealt with yourself and can advise me on.'

When the others had gone, he said, 'Do you want to ring home and say you'll be out for lunch?'

'But you're going out to dinner tonight,' she reminded him. 'You won't want to lunch out as well.'

'Certainly I do. I'll be getting the car out. You know where the phone is…by the sofa in the living room.'

Her parents' phone was in answerphone mode. She left a message. Then she went into the hall just as Nicolás was coming through the front door.

'All OK? Good. Let's go. I'm blocking the street,' he said briskly.

It was Cally's first experience of being a passenger in a luxurious car with leather upholstery and a woodgrain dashboard. To her surprise, instead of going the way she expected, he took the opposite direction which involved negotiating an opening between two houses that was scarcely wider than his car. The slightest misjudgment would have resulted in a scrape on the car's coachwork. Using his wing mirrors as skilfully as Mog used his whiskers, Nicolás steered the car through the narrow gap as if he had been driving around the backways of small villages all his life.

Crossing the *plana* in his car was not the bumpy progress it was in her mother's car. His car's suspension made it feel more like gliding across the Venetian lagoon in a motorboat as she and Olivia and Deborah had one memorable weekend a couple of years ago when Deborah had booked them on a 'great bargain offer' flight.

'Have you been to Venice?' she asked.

'Of course. It's one of life's essential experiences, don't you think?'

'I've only been there once, but yes I do…think it's essential, I mean. If I were a millionaire, I would have a house there.'

'Where would you have your other houses?' he asked, with a smiling glance at her.

'I don't know. I haven't travelled as much as I should like to. The house in Chelsea where I have a bedsit is great, and I'd always want a pad in Spain. Where would you want to have bases if you were fabulously rich?'

* * *

At that moment, at the wheel of another beautiful car, His Excellency the Marqués de Mondragón was saying to his wife, 'Nicolás's latest poppet seems a nice girl. What did you think of her?'

'I liked her,' said Cassia. 'But I'm not sure they're on those terms. What makes you think so?'

'Just his track record with women, I guess. I've never heard him called a womaniser, but if he fancies someone I'm told they usually succumb. Unlike his brother, Nicolás is popular with everyone, always has been. It's a pity he's not the heir. He might have pulled that family back on track which an effete ass like Rodrigo, who takes after their mother, will never do.'

'From all I've heard about her, I should think the *duquesa* would be a ghastly mother-in-law,' said Cassia. 'Your mother rarely says a bad word about anyone, but I know she dislikes the *duquesa*. Nicolás must take after his father. He's the one who's a diplomat, isn't he?'

'Yes, an ambassador...due to retire pretty soon, I should imagine. He was the best of her husbands and Nicolás is the best of her children. He's a clever guy. Did Cally strike you as up to his weight?'

'Hard to tell on so short an acquaintance. But clever men don't necessarily need clever wives. I'm not up to your weight intellectually, but you seem to be content with me.'

Mondragón took a hand off the wheel and reached for one of her hands. 'I adore you, and you know it,' he said, kissing her fingers. 'If we have a daughter with as good a brain as her mother, and better opportunities than you had, in twenty-five years from now she'll be one of Spain's outstanding career women.'

'I hope she manages to combine it with being someone's happy wife,' said Cassia. 'If I'd been at university, instead of working as a receptionist, I wouldn't have met you.' After a pause, she added, 'When Nicolás comes to dinner tonight,

I'll ask him about her. You can always tell when a man is serious about a girl by the way he talks about her.'

'I doubt if that applies to Nicolás,' said her husband. 'He has always kept his cards very close to his chest. It was a surprise to everyone when he suddenly emerged as one of the leaders of the IT industry and, although his mother and sisters are frequently in *Hola!*, you'll never see him there. He knows how to guard his privacy.'

'The house was called La Soledad,' said Nicolás, as he drove through a gap in the trees and the building came into view.

Occasionally Cally had seen other houses of this type, relics of Spain's nineteenth-century past, sometimes standing in the middle of extensive orange or olive groves. In England they would be called manor houses, not as large and grand as stately homes, but still important focal points of rural life.

Inside the surrounding ring of trees, a yellow digger had been at work clearing undergrowth and saplings. But today it was standing idle and there seemed to be no one else about.

As they left the car and walked towards the main entrance, she looked up at the façade and saw places where seeds had blown into crevices in the stucco and grown into plants, causing a network of cracks in the surrounding service.

Yet, despite its neglected state, the house did not look depressing. Perhaps it would in a different climate but here, under a blue sky and hot sun, it looked a romantic ruin.

'Are you going to have it photographed as it is now?' she asked. 'After you've done it up, it would be interesting to have a record of how it was.'

'I agree. It has already been done...by me and by a professional photographer my architect recommended. I used a digital camera. Next time you're at my place I'll show you the results.'

He unlocked the great door and pushed it open, its hinges creaking. They entered a large hall with a wide staircase curving upwards to the floor above.

'It smelled a lot worse the first time I came,' said Nicolás. 'Since then I've spent a day here with all the shutters and windows open to give it an airing.'

They wandered from room to room. Cally said, 'I wonder what it was like in its heyday. Do you suppose there are photographs of it in old forgotten albums?'

'Maybe. I'll have a look some time.'

Presently, he unlocked a door at the rear of the house that led out to what had once been a formal garden. Elaborate urns set on the tops of pillars marked flights of shallow steps.

Cally was sauntering down one of these, a little ahead of Nicolás, when what she had thought was a stick suddenly started to move. The realisation that it was a large dark snake made her gasp and jump back, catching her heel on one of the steps behind her and losing her footing.

If Nicolás hadn't been watching and grabbed her, she would have fallen. He shot out his hands and caught her around the lower part of her ribcage, or at least that was his intention. But as she lurched sideways, arms flailing in a vain attempt to recover her balance, his right hand covered her right breast.

'It was only a ladder snake…not venomous. The sun brought him out,' said Nicolás, shifting his hand to her midriff and holding her steady.

And then, while she was still reeling mentally, not so much from the shock of the snake as from the electric sensation of his hand on her breast, he turned her around and drew her against him and kissed her.

CHAPTER EIGHT

As SHE had the first time he kissed her, Cally forgot everything but her need to be in his arms.

She responded as freely and eagerly as she had the first time, perhaps even more ardently now she knew she was in love with him.

Whatever restraint her brain might impose—but for the moment it was switched off—her body had longed for these moments. His mouth was like water in the desert, the feel of his body against hers like food after starvation.

When at last they stopped kissing and looked into each other's eyes, Nicolás said huskily, 'What this garden needs is a summer house with an ample supply of cushions. If it had somewhere private and comfortable, would you say no to me this time? Now that we know each other better?'

Cally leaned back in the circle of his arms. She put hands on either side of his face and caressed the slanting cheekbones and the taut brown skin with her fingertips.

'But still not well enough for that. I would like you to make love to me. I can't deny it. But the last time it happened, I regretted it later. How do I know I wouldn't regret it this time? It's a gamble, and I'm not a gambler.'

He captured one of her hands and pressed his mouth to the palm. Then he dropped his arm from around her and stepped back.

'I think we had better go and have lunch and talk about this unsuccessful relationship that seems to have put you off trying again. But first I must lock up here. Come—' He took her by the hand, as he might have done with a child, and led her back to the house.

* * *

Half an hour later he parked the car outside a *bar-restaurante* in a hamlet of perhaps twenty houses on a mountain road with a view of the coast.

The only other customers were an elderly couple sitting outside under a striped sunbrella and six Spanish workmen at one of the inside tables.

Nicolás chose an outside table as far away from the other couple as possible. After they had decided what to eat from the simple menu, and a bottle of wine had been brought and their glasses filled, he said, 'Now tell me the story of your love life?'

'There isn't very much to tell. A friend had a bad experience that put me off experimenting when I was in my teens. When I was twenty I fell in love...or what seemed to be love. It wasn't. It was also a disaster sexually,' she said bluntly. 'After that I decided there was a lot to be said for being celibate.'

Having described two years of increasing anguish in the baldest possible terms, she held her breath, dreading him telling her that her lover had been a dolt and he, Nicolás, was an expert lover who would make the experience perfect for her.

To her infinite relief, he didn't do that.

He said, 'What sort of bad experience did your friend have?'

'She was very pretty and had lots of boyfriends. She caught herpes simplex. Although it was treated, it's been recurring ever since. Sometimes it never recurs. Sometimes it does apparently. She's been told that if she has a baby, she will have to have it by Caesarian section to avoid infecting it.'

Nicolás said, 'Teenage promiscuity carries some nasty penalties. Nobody denies that. But that doesn't mean that making love is always like Russian roulette, Cally.

Intelligent adults can give each other pleasure without those kinds of consequences.'

'I expect they can,' she agreed. 'But men can take pleasure for granted. Woman can't. You may be an exceptionally good lover…or you may be like the previous man in my life. It's not a chance I'm prepared to take…except under certain conditions which don't apply in our case.'

'What conditions?' he asked.

She drank some wine, choosing her words carefully. 'If I loved someone, and he loved me, then I would chance it. Not otherwise. Sex is rather like chocolate…a moment on the lips, a lifetime on the hips. Sometimes it's hard to resist transient pleasures. But I think it pays off in the long run.'

He leaned back in his chair, his expression thoughtful. 'I think you may be allowing two bad experiences—your friend's and your own—to warp your judgment. Life is about embracing experience, not rejecting it. This guy who was your first lover…was he also a virgin?'

'I don't know. I shouldn't think so. He was twenty-three.'

'Did you tell him he was leaving you cold? Not as bluntly as that, but tactfully?'

'I felt that if he didn't know, there wasn't much point in telling him.'

'So you lay back and thought of England, as the saying goes. Where does that expression come from?'

'I'm not sure. I'll look it up. Which reminds me, that website address you sent me, as an example that Edmund & Burke ought to copy…how do you come to know about Harlequin romances? Does one of your sisters read them?'

'As far as I know my sisters never read anything but fashion magazines. I was introduced to Harlequin books in San Francisco at an Internet conference. I heard some of the women delegates discussing the fact that, in the city's financial sector, there were special jackets on sale so that women business executives could read a romance in public without other people knowing. I don't know why they would feel embarrassed about it. If men want to read John Grisham or Stephen King, they do it and don't care who knows it.'

'It's a man's world,' said Cally. 'For some reason, stories involving crime and violence are more socially acceptable than stories about emotional relationships.'

'Do you read romances in secret as a substitute for the real thing?' he asked her.

She said lightly, 'I seldom read novels of any kind…and I haven't given up hope that "the real thing" will happen eventually. Which is one of the reasons I'm not going to have an affair with you, Nicolás. If and when my Mr Right materialises, I believe he'll be pleased that I waited for him. Think about it. When you marry, do you want your wife to have a long line of lovers in her past? Be honest.'

At this point their salads arrived, with a basket of bread and a yellow pottery bowl filled with *alioli*.

When they were alone again, Nicolás said, 'It would be unreasonable to expect my future wife to have a past far more immaculate than mine. For both sexes, there's a difference between being promiscuous and having relationships that, although not permanent, do involve real liking and affection. Post-marital fidelity is a lot more important than pre-marital abstinence. I think you may be using Mr Right as an excuse to avoid having to use your judgment…having made an error of judgment before.'

'But I *am* using my judgment,' she objected. 'I've admitted…demonstrated that I find you attractive. But reason tells me it would be a mistake to go beyond friendship. Hopefully, I'm not going to be here for much longer. There was a job for a commissioning editor on one of the book trade press sites this morning. With a bit of luck I may get it and then I'll being going back to London and our paths won't cross any more…or only rarely.'

'London isn't far by air. I go there several times a year.'

'So you may, but when people are based in different countries there's no point in getting involved...unless they're both mad about each other, and we aren't,' she said firmly. 'Tell me more about your friends. What does he do for a living, and why was she living in Granada when they met?'

'Simón's involved in the management of land and property,' said Nicolás. 'Cassia's father was a painter and the narrow streets and stairways of the Albaicin have always attracted artists. If you had accepted their invitation to dinner, she would have told you how they met. Were you telling the truth about Juanita not being able to stand in for you, or was that a polite excuse?'

'I felt I would be an interloper,' she admitted. 'You've known them a long time and have lots of things in common.'

'I don't know Cassia well. You would have been someone for her to talk to while I asked Simón for advice. You have far more in common with her than I do. Why not change your mind and come?'

Cally hesitated. Then common sense reminded her that, although there might be no harm in going out to dinner with him, the drive home could be hazardous. If he kissed her goodnight, her resolution might weaken. She might find herself in his bed instead of her own.

It was hard to be strong-minded in daylight, and much harder late at night.

'I would rather not,' she said quietly but firmly.

Nicolás made a very Spanish gesture expressing a mixture of bafflement and resignation. Changing the subject, he said, 'If I hadn't had a project of my own for La Soledad, I might have sold it to Simón for his children's scheme. He wants to expand it, but suitable properties aren't easy to come by.'

For the rest of the meal, they discussed impersonal topics.

On the drive back to Valdecarrasca, they hardly spoke, both immersed in their private thoughts.

Cally was wondering if she had done a foolish thing in rejecting Nicolás's advances. He wanted her. She wanted him. Was it madness to turn down the chance to erase for ever the memory of her earlier affair?

There was no real doubt in her mind that he would be a much better lover than clueless Andrew. It would be impossible not to be. Even the way Nicolás kissed and held her was different.

Knowing he would have his full attention on the bends of the winding mountain road, she shot a sideways glance at him, remembering the feel of his face under her fingers.

How lovely it would be if they were going back to his house for a shared *'siesta'*.

She remembered the old man who had spoken to her this morning. *Enjoy being young while you can. Before you know it, you'll be as old as I am.* Already she was halfway through her twenties. Before long she would be a thirty-something, with no possibility of meeting a man to compare with the one beside her.

She wondered how he would react if she suddenly announced a change of mind. But even after the mid-morning glass of champagne and another two glasses of wine with lunch, she didn't have the courage to say, 'I've been thinking it over. If you want me, you can have me.'

Nicolás, though he was driving with the care the road demanded, was also mentally reviewing the way he had, for the second time, mishandled his relationship with Cally.

Both times he had been too precipitate for a woman who was like no other he had ever met.

He was both touched and exasperated by her determination to forego the best and most important of all the sensual pleasures until the mythical Mr Right came along. Presumably, despite her close associations with Spain, she saw Mr Right as an Englishman.

He knew and liked a number of Englishmen though, in general, he had more in common with Americans with their can-do attitudes and openness to innovation. Among the European nations, he saw Spain as being in the ascendant and Britain as being in decline, a state that befell all imperial powers eventually. It had happened to the Greeks and the Romans, and to Spain as well, centuries earlier.

Glancing at Cally's averted face as she gazed out of the window, he wondered what she was thinking about and if she was now determined never to let him lay a finger on her again.

Earlier today it had been in his mind to ask her to join him on his Christmas trip to the Ariège, a beautiful and relatively undiscovered region of France to the north of the Pyrenees. A friend of his had been there and reported simple but good accommodation and one or two excellent restaurants.

Staying there with Cally, walking in the foothills by day, and sharing a duvet by night, would have been good for them both.

Unfortunately he had muffed his chance of achieving that objective when they were in the garden at La Soledad. The snake had presented him with the opportunity to hold her—his palm still held the memory of her softness—and instead of being content with that for the time being, he had gone too far. Referring to what they might have done in a non-existent summer house had been a tactical error, conjuring up images that, for her, had unpleasant associations. Whoever the lout was who had botched her initiation deserved to be shot. No wonder she was nervous of being let down again.

Nicolás had never felt protective towards a woman before, except in the ordinary way of carrying things for the elderly and intervening if small boys were too rough in their dealings with small girls. It seemed to him that most females between those extremes could look after themselves pretty well. Certainly all the women in his family could, and none of his girlfriends had shown any sign of vulnerability.

Cally was different. As far as he could make out, she had spent most of her life looking after her parents instead of being cherished by them. That she should have to spend Christmas being a general factotum, instead of having a good time with her contemporaries, annoyed him intensely.

He wondered how much interest her parents took in her job problems, and if they were secretly hoping that she wouldn't be able to get another job as an editor and could be persuaded to run the *casa rural* on a permanent basis, leaving them free to play golf and bridge.

'If you'll drop me off at the corner by the school, that will be fine,' said Cally, as they neared the village. 'Thank you very much for lunch, Nicolás. It was a nice place. I'll pin the flyer the owner gave me on our noticeboard. Some of our guests may want to try it.'

He did as she suggested, stopping the car near Valdecarrasca's school and jumping out to walk round the bonnet and open the passenger's door for her. But Cally was already on her feet when he reached the car's nearside.

'I hope you enjoy your evening. Thanks again for my lunch.' She gave him an artificially bright smile because, inwardly, she felt close to tears.

After today, he would probably never want to see her again. What man would, after such an emphatic rejection?

'My pleasure. We must do it again,' said Nicolás.

But she felt sure it was just a polite form of words. He couldn't possibly mean it.

*   *   *

The next day Cally paid a visit to Dolores Martinez's grandmother to ask her about her time as a kitchen maid at La Soledad.

As Spanish country people regarded bunches of flowers as tributes to take to the cemetery, not as social offerings, she took a box of chocolates.

The old lady was in bed, propped up by pillows, wearing a black crocheted wool shawl over her nightdress. People of her generation, and indeed many of the over-sixties, went into mourning for husbands and other close relations for at least a year and sometimes for the rest of their lives.

After some preliminary politenesses, Cally began by saying, in Valenciano, 'I've heard that, when you were a girl, you worked at the big house called Solitude on the other side of the valley. Can you remember what it was like in those days?'

The old lady's face lit up, perhaps with pleasure at being invited to reminisce. 'I remember it well…better than I can remember what happened last year,' she said, her smile displaying the many gaps among her teeth. 'Every year is the same now, but when I was young there was always something happening. I don't know why they called the house Solitude. It was always full of people when the family came from Madrid. They were a big family and often their friends came as well. They had motor cars before anyone else…'

Once launched, she was unstoppable. Cally wished she had had the forethought to bring her microcassette recorder. She was not going to be able to remember every detail. The story the old lady was telling was a fascinating insight into the social life of a grand family as glimpsed by one of the youngest and least important members of the household.

After about half an hour, she suddenly fell asleep. When it seemed she was not going to wake up for some time, Cally tiptoed from the room and asked the granddaughter if she could come again another day.

'Certainly…whenever you please. It's nice for her to have company. We've all heard her tales a thousand times,' said Señora Martinez, with a gesture expressing extreme boredom.

As soon as she got home, Cally typed as much as she could remember of the old lady's reminiscences. She badly needed something to take her mind off her two major problems: being out of work and in love with Nicolás. Working on a piece of social history would give her something else to think about. It was even possible that, suitably edited, the reminiscences might be saleable, or at least worth preserving in a local history archive.

She was picking up emails that evening when the name Nicolás Llorca appeared, the subject of the message being *Party*.

Cally opened it and read—*I want to return the Drydens' hospitality before I go away for the holiday period. I'm having a party on Constitucion Española. I hope you and your parents can come. 8.30 p.m. Nicolás*

Spanish Constitution day was the first of two national *fiestas* that took place early in December, the second being to celebrate the Immaculate Conception.

The invitation surprised her. She thought she had seen and heard the last of Nicolás, apart from possible chance encounters in the street. She was also surprised that he had included her parents in the invitation. Although he had never been anything but polite to them, intuition told her he didn't like them, though the reason for his antipathy was something she couldn't fathom.

For her own peace of mind, she was tempted to invent an excuse for declining the invitation without telling her parents about it. But then she realised it could lead to one of those 'tangled web' situations that were better not embarked on.

Having relayed the invitation to them, she replied to his

email. *Thank you, we'd all be delighted to come to your party.*

That evening she was called to the telephone by her mother. With her hand over the mouthpiece, Mrs Haig said, 'It's someone called Luis. He wants your London telephone number.'

'Luis?' Cally said blankly.

Then she remembered the art dealer she had met at the Drydens' party. All that had happened since then had erased him from her memory.

Taking the receiver from her mother, she said, 'Hello, Luis…how are you?'

'I'm fine…all the better for hearing that you're here, not in London. I'm going to be in London in the New Year and I wanted to ring you to ask if you would have lunch or dinner with me. But as you are here and I shall be driving from Valencia to Alicante tomorrow, perhaps I could have the pleasure of your company sooner than I'd hoped. There's a restaurant at the south end of Benissa that's not at all bad. I've eaten there before.'

Before she had time to reply, he said, 'I have something *very* interesting to tell you about a mutual acquaintance.'

The only mutual acquaintances Cally could think of were the Drydens.

But then Luis added, 'The good-looking guy who was at our table at Leonora's dinner party.'

'Nicolás Llorca?'

'Yes, Llorca. But don't ask me to tell you what I've found out about him over the phone. The price of this information—which, believe me, would make headlines in *Información* if they knew about his presence in your village—is the pleasure of your company at lunch. All I will say now is that the way he described himself when we introduced ourselves was the most stupendous understatement I've ever heard.'

Cally did not like being pressured into having lunch with a man whom, though she had found his company quite agreeable, she had no real desire to meet again. At the same time she was intensely curious to know what information he had unearthed about Nicolás.

He was waiting for her when she arrived at their rendezvous in a town on the main coast road.

'What takes you to Alicante?' she asked, when they were settled at a table. 'An art exhibition?'

Luis nodded. 'I've been invited to the inauguration party for an art festival at the Castle of Santa Barbara. I'll drive home tomorrow, or perhaps the day after. I thought you'd be back in Spain for Christmas, but not as soon as this.'

'I'm changing jobs,' she said. 'My new one doesn't start until the New Year.' She felt the white lie was allowable. She didn't want to discuss her job situation with him.

Nicolás wasn't mentioned until they had finished the main course and were waiting for the pudding.

'You have your curiosity under very good control,' he said. 'Most women would have asked me what I've found out long before now.'

'Perhaps I'm not curious,' she said. 'What made you think I would need a bait to have lunch with you?'

'Because I have no illusions about my powers of attraction,' he said, rather sadly. 'I am not in Llorca's league. He can have any woman he wants.'

'I doubt that,' she said dryly. 'What makes you think so?'

'His looks, his personality…and the fact that he's a billionaire.'

'He may be very well off, but a billionaire… I don't believe it.'

'*Time* magazine does. They've published a profile of him, and they don't do that for every Internet whizz-kid. I asked a librarian I know to do some ''digging'' for me. The stuff he came up with was an eye-opener. The service provider Llorca mentioned is only one of his enterprises. In the last ten years he's launched half a dozen companies, the most recent being a fibre optic network that will link most of Spain's larger cities by a voice and data network. I don't understand the technicalities of that but perhaps you do.'

Cally shook her head. 'Only dimly.'

'Apparently Llorca has been a speaker at most of the international economic forums. He's an innovator…a force to be reckoned with.'

'Did you find out why he's spending time in this part of Spain?'

'No, I didn't,' said Luis. 'Either it's something personal or it's not in the public domain yet. Have you seen any more of him since the dinner party?'

She hesitated. 'We've had lunch, but I don't expect to see him again.'

'Probably better not to,' said Luis. 'People like Llorca are not like the rest of us. I've known several of those ''driving force'' types and they're not good at personal relationships. They're too ambitious…too focused. They tend to have serial marriages or a string of mistresses.'

'You don't have to warn me off, Luis. I'm not an impressionable twenty-year-old, and I'm well aware that Nicolás inhabits a different world from the one I live in.' She changed the subject. 'Have you discovered any up-and-coming new artists recently?'

In the light of Luis's information, Cally regretted even more that she hadn't declined the invitation to Nicolás's party.

'I wonder who's cooking for him?' said Mrs Haig, as she and her husband and daughter were about to set out for La Higuera. 'Juanita says someone called Alicia looked after the place when Cameron Fielding was a bachelor. But I don't know if she does now. I gather Juanita and Alicia aren't on good terms. She didn't say why, but I knew by her expression she doesn't think much of Alicia.'

Cally made no comment. She was increasingly nervous about the evening ahead. Would her father drink too much? Would her mother choose tonight to air some of her more extreme views? Why was it so important to her that they made a good impression? If she were a truly loving daughter she would be more concerned about whether they liked the other people, not vice versa. That was how she would have felt if her grandmother had been going to the party. But it wasn't the way she felt about Mum and Dad. With them it was she who felt like a parent with two children who might behave perfectly…or throw embarrassing tantrums.

Her hope that all would be well rose when her father said to her mother, 'You look very nice tonight, dear. Is that a new dress?'

But then, instead of making the most of one of his rare compliments, her mother spoiled it by saying tartly, 'That'll be the day. It must be at least ten years old. Shows how much notice you take.'

'You know men don't notice details, Mum,' Cally said quickly. 'They take in the general impression, and you are looking nice tonight.'

Mrs Haig gave one of her sniffs and Cally's nervousness increased. It was going to be stressful enough, being with Nicolás and trying not to remember what had happened at La Soledad, without having to keep a watchful eye on these two as well.

As they were turning into the street where Nicolás lived, they had to step onto the narrow pavement to allow a car to pass. It was an expensive car and Cally wondered if the couple in it were also bound for La Higuera.

It turned out they were. By the time the Haigs reached the front door, the Spanish couple were also approaching it. The man was still handsome despite being considerably overweight and the woman was fashionably coiffed and wearing a fur coat, furs not being frowned on in Spain.

They were introduced by the husband as Enrique and Angeles Gonzalez. Knowing that her father wouldn't, Cally introduced her parents and herself. They were still shaking hands when Nicolás, who must have heard the car draw up, opened the door to welcome them.

The Drydens had already arrived and, after further introductions, the three male guests formed a group, and the three older women another, while Nicolás handed round flutes of champagne and Cally gazed at a wonderful painting which now filled the formerly empty space on the chimney-breast.

'Is that a Sorolla?' she asked, as he brought her a glass.

'Yes…do you like it?'

'It's beautiful. I like all his paintings, especially *El Caballo Blanco*…a naked boy in a straw hat leading a white horse out of the sea.'

'This picture used to hang in the drawing room at La Soledad. I shall probably put it back there when the place is habitable again.' He turned to speak to her mother. 'You were away when I spent a night or two at your house, Mrs Haig. Have you had any news about the man who had to be taken to hospital?'

'We've heard he's made a good recovery.' After they had been chatting for a few minutes, she said, 'Can we do anything to help? Entertaining is difficult for a man on his own.'

'Thank you, but no, everything's under control. I've found an excellent caterer who came in earlier today and left me with nothing to do but open the bottles. Excuse me'—this as someone rang the front doorbell.

Moments later he returned with two more guests, the couple Cally had met at the arts and crafts fair. Tonight Simón's English wife was looking even more beautiful in a loose beaded chiffon top and plain silk trousers, both the colour of violets. As soon as the introductions had been made, she made a bee-line for Cally.

'I was hoping you might be here. We go back to Madrid tomorrow and I wanted to see you again.'

Touched by the warmth of her manner, Cally responded equally warmly.

As his email hadn't stated what form the evening would take, she had wondered if 'a party' meant only *tapas* and drinks or something more substantial. But when Nicolás folded back the doors that had closed off the seating area, she saw that the table was laid as for a dinner party and the long counter that partially divided the dining and cooking areas had been converted into a buffet with an inviting array of food.

If her father had been the host, where people sat would have been left to chance. But place cards indicated that Nicolás had worked out a plan. When everyone was sitting down, her mother was on his right with Mrs Dryden on his left.

At the other end of the table was Cassia Mondragón with Mr Haig on her right and Todd Dryden on her left. Cally was between Enrique and Mr Dryden with Angeles opposite her.

All three were good conversationalists and presently she began to relax and enjoy herself, though she couldn't help keeping a watchful eye on her father and wondering how her mother was getting on with their host and Leonora Dryden.

It was soon agreed that the caterer Nicolás had used was a notable find. The starters included a curried courgette soup on a hot-plate, salmon fishcakes also hot, a Brie tart and a green salad made with celery, cucumber, endive and lettuce heart leaves to which had been added walnuts, pickled garlic and the baby gherkins called *pepinillos*.

It was when dinner was over and Nicolás and Simón were serving coffee and liqueurs to the older members of the party, now relaxing on the comfortable sofas in the living area, that Cassia said to her host, 'I love looking round other people's houses. Is it all right if Cally and I have a snoop?'

'Of course…look wherever you like.'

As they went into the hall, Cassia said, 'First, I must have a *pipi*. What's the betting that door at the end is the down-stairs loo?'

While she was gone, Cally looked at the paintings and photographs on the walls in the hall. Although she didn't watch much TV, she had seen Cameron Fielding, the owner of the house, and knew that he had reported the news from many parts of the world. His paintings and other possessions reflected his nomadic life and reminded Cally that Cassia had also described herself as a nomad before meeting Simón.

She learned some more about Cassia as they explored the house and, when an opportunity arose, she said, 'The other day someone told me that Nicolás is rather more famous than he lets on.'

'Oh, yes, in his field he's a big name,' Cassia agreed, 'but you wouldn't guess it from his manner. He never flaunts his brains. Simón has a lot of time for him.'

This, Cally gathered, was the ultimate accolade in Cassia's eyes.

'Do you like him?' she asked.

'I haven't known him long but, yes, he seems very nice,' Cally said, thinking that her answer had to be the under-statement of the year. She wondered what Cassia would say if she confided that she was hopelessly in love with him.

The Haigs were the first to leave.

'Did you enjoy yourself?' Cally asked her mother, as they walked home.

'I'd like to know what that buffet cost,' said Mrs Haig. 'There was a lot left over. We could have done with doggy bags. I hate to see good food wasted.'

Cally smothered a sigh. Her mother's comments were so typical of her. After spending an enjoyable evening in a lovely house among interesting people, all her reactions were negative. How differently darling Granny would have reacted.

Aloud, she said, 'I'm sure it won't be. Nicolás will eat what was left.'

She felt sure that he would. Billionaire or not, she couldn't see him tossing eatable food into the garbage.

'Leonora Dryden is a very amusing woman. I wasn't much taken with Mrs Haig. She has a discontented mouth,' said Simón, driving away from Valdecarrasca.

'Perhaps that's her husband's fault. His only topic is golf. Luckily I had Todd on my other side and he's great fun,' said Cassia. 'Cally can't help having dull parents,' she added. 'She must be a changeling or a throwback. We found we had lots of favourite books in common. But I didn't pick up any clues about how she feels about Nicolás.'

'I didn't see any evidence to support your theory about his feelings,' said her husband. 'The fact that he never mentioned her the evening he came to supper with us would suggest to me that he wasn't interested. How you can interpret that as a sign that he's in love with her is beyond me.'

'But then you didn't have a clue that I was in love with you, my dense darling,' said Cassia. 'Men are hopeless at picking up vibes. Of course it's never as easy when one is an interested party,' she conceded. 'I didn't guess that you were in love with me. Maybe I'm wrong about Nicolás. Maybe he only fancies her in a love 'em and leave 'em way.'

CHAPTER NINE

AT BREAKFAST the following morning, Leonora said to her husband, 'I have a sinking feeling that Cally has fallen for Nicolás.'

'He probably has a lot of girls falling for him. What makes you think she has?'

'I intercepted some looks she gave him…and he her. But if they have an affair, she's the one who will be hurt when it ends.'

'She's a nice girl. Maybe it won't end,' said Todd. Talking to Cally the night before had led him to believe she had a lot going for her.

'He won't marry her,' said Leonora. 'Just because one of the Spanish princesses has married a basketball player, it doesn't mean that the entire Spanish aristocracy is going to start marrying commoners. Mostly they'll stick to their own kind.'

'I doubt if Nicolás thinks of himself as an aristocrat, first and foremost, and his mother certainly hasn't observed the conventions,' said Todd. '*La duquesa* is notorious for her liaisons with unsuitable partners.'

'The children of people like that often react to their parents' peccadilloes by becoming extremely conventional,' said Leonora. 'Augustus John—' referring to one of her favourite artists '—was a complete bohemian, but his son joined the Royal Navy and became an admiral. Do you remember John's beautiful illegitimate daughter, Amaryllis Fleming? We went to one of her concerts soon after we were married.'

'The red-head who played the cello…yes, I remember

her. Wasn't she related to the guy who wrote the James Bond books?'

'She was Ian Fleming's half-sister,' said Leonora. 'Her mother was like Nicolás's mother…madly attractive and notorious for the number of her lovers. I suppose it's possible that Nicolás, despite his looks and charm, could, by temperament, be more suited to the role of a faithful husband than a successful womaniser. But I shouldn't like to bet on it and, given his eligibility, I think he's unlikely to pick someone like Cally. She's what I call a connoisseur's beauty, and he may recognise that, but she's also encumbered with terribly tedious parents. Mrs Haig has one of the most pedestrian minds I've ever encountered.'

'Your parents were an odd pair, but I took the chance that you wouldn't turn out like them,' her husband reminded her teasingly.

Leonora laughed. 'I doubt if Nicolás is as reckless as you were. Men who've stayed single till his age don't embark on marriage as lightly as we, who married in our twenties, did.'

The letter from London was delivered by Juan the *cartero* who, unlike British postmen, did not have a uniform and drive an official van, but wore a sweater or, rarely, an anorak, and drove his own car.

If he had a package to deliver to the *casa rural*, he would open the door and put the mail on a nearby table. This morning he rang the bell because he needed a signature for an expensive laid-paper envelope sent by registered post.

Stamped on the flap at the back was a name that made Cally's heart leap. Founded in 1784, Quarles & Co (Publishers) Ltd was one of the last surviving independent publishing houses in London, with a reputation for finely produced scholarly books.

The letter inside was typewritten but topped and tailed

with the elegant handwriting of someone who used a fountain pen.

Dear Miss Haig, she read—the writer obviously didn't consider Ms an acceptable form of address—*We have been offered the opening chapters and an outline of a book by Mr Rhys McGregor. We are interested in seeing more of this work and have been in correspondence with the author who tells us...*

Cally read to the end of the first sheet and turned to the next. The letter was signed by Robert Quarles, whom she knew was a descendant of the founder, and who had 'Editor: General Books Division' typed under his unusually legible signature. What it boiled down to was that Rhys had told them about the situation at Edmund & Burke and that he wanted to change his publisher but not his editor.

This was a bold proviso for a one-book author to make and might not have cut any ice but for the fact that the chairman's wife, Lady Quarles, had received *River of Life, Death and Love* as a birthday present and recommended the book to her husband. Also the company was unexpectedly losing one of its editors. In short, they would like to interview Cally with a view to offering her a post and Rhys a contract.

For some minutes Cally was in heaven. Working for Quarles would be a dream come true. She had often passed their premises in Dover Street and longed to see the famous drawing room where, for more than two centuries, some of the greatest names in English literature had been entertained.

Then, abruptly, she came down to earth. If she got the job, it would mean going back to London, never seeing Nicolás again, or only at infrequent intervals when her visits to her parents coincided with his visits to La Soledad. Which wouldn't be often and might be never.

Common sense dictated that she rang up Robert Quarles's secretary and arranged an appointment for the following week. Then she emailed Rhys to congratulate him on exciting their interest in his new book and to thank him for insisting she should edit it. The fact that Edmund & Burke had not offered him a two-or three-book contract had been a disappointment at the time but, as matters had turned out, was proving to be an advantage. Finally, she booked a flight to London.

The night before she left, Nicolás rang up.

'There's something I'd like to discuss with you. Will you come here or shall I come there? Or shall we meet in the bar?'

'We'll have to sit outside. At this time of night with the TV blaring and the bar full, we shouldn't be able to hear ourselves speak,' she said.

'I can wrap up warmly if you can. How about half an hour's time?'

Cally agreed and rang off, wondering what he could possibly want to talk about.

He was there before her, a bottle of wine and two glasses already on the table.

As they sat down he wasted no time in coming to the point. 'If you're still in need of a job, I have one to offer you. We shall be needing an editor to knock the text for our website and courses into shape. Not many people with technical expertise are good at communicating their ideas. You're ideally qualified to handle the job we want done.'

It was on the tip of her tongue to tell him about the Quarles job interview, but she decided not to. 'When would you want me to start, and how long would the job last?'

'In about a month's time and we'd offer you a contract for a year which, all being well, would be renewed for a further year.'

'Can I have a little time to think about it?'

'I'll give you a week,' said Nicolás, pouring out wine.

'You would have to come to Madrid and meet some of my colleagues before we signed you up.'

'What I'm not clear about is when what you've called your "centre of excellence" is going to be open for business. Even with a topnotch architect supervising the works, I should have thought it could take a long time to put La Soledad in order.'

'It probably will,' he said easily. 'Until it's ready, you may have to work in several places. Here…in Madrid…and possibly even in the US. That won't bother you, will it? You won't have to worry about accommodation. We'll organise that for you.'

'No, moving about wouldn't worry me. I've been doing it all my life. Their six years in Valdecarrasca is the longest time my parents have stayed put anywhere,' she said dryly.

'Do you think they are fixed here? Have they had enough moving?'

'I hope so…but who knows?'

'Perhaps you worry about them too much? They're only in their fifties, not on the verge of decrepitude.'

'Do you never worry about your parents?'

'Never,' he said emphatically. 'In fact I don't worry about anything very much. There's no point in it. If there's a problem and I can deal with it, I do. I don't believe in losing sleep, the way a lot of people do, over things that may never happen.'

'They probably don't have your confidence that they can handle everything life may throw at them. You're in control of your life. Most people aren't.'

'Nobody's totally in control of their lives, Cally. Accidents happen. Illnesses happen. Meanwhile one trusts to luck.' He leaned towards her, smiling. 'You haven't asked what most people would consider the key question about a new job.'

'I haven't?' she said, in a puzzled tone.

'The salary. Don't you want to know what the pay is?'

Feeling foolish, she said, 'I suppose, when you're out of work, you don't worry about the pay as much as people who are in work and can pick and choose about moving. What is the salary you're offering?'

When he told her, she was surprised. It was more than she had been earning at Edmund & Burke by a substantial amount.

'If we find that you suit us, and the job suits you, there will also be some stock options,' said Nicolás. 'That's normal in Internet technology industries. People with a stake in a business are more willing to put in long hours and give their best.'

Cally was beginning to feel that she ought to tell him about the Quarles interview. But as he had given her a week to think about his offer, she decided not to mention it.

'And there's one other thing I should tell you,' said Nicolás, refilling their glasses. 'If you decide to join Llorca Enterprises, you can take it as read that the boss won't be making any passes at you. Our relationship will be strictly businesslike. I mention it because there may be times when we have to travel together and perhaps spend nights in hotels. I have absolutely no ulterior motive in offering this post to you, Cally. I hope you believe that.'

'Of course... I never thought otherwise. You aren't the sort of person who would trade on anyone's vulnerabilities.' But, even as she said it, she felt a sinking of the heart because, if she took the job, it would mean that he would regard her as for ever off-limits.

'You didn't always have such a high opinion of me,' he said, looking amused.

She was saved from answering by the arrival of one of Valdecarrasca's least prosperous inhabitants, a man who earned his living as a labourer on roadworks. He greeted Cally politely, but was more familiar with Nicolás, joshing him about his running. Nicolás took his remarks in good part and, after a bit more banter, the man gave him a friendly thump on the shoulder and disappeared into the bar for his nightly *quinto* of beer.

It struck Cally that only someone whose success and wealth had had no effect on his sense of self-importance would have responded as Nicolás had. The more she knew of him, the more she admired his character. In the world of publishers, authors and literary agents there were many inflated egos. She had always warmed to people who, despite outstanding achievements, had remained unspoiled and unpretentious.

'By the way, I have ordered several copies of the book you edited, *River of Life, Death and Love*, for people I think would enjoy it, one of them being Cassia,' said Nicolás. 'She has always wanted to go to India.'

'So have I,' said Cally. 'Have you been?'

'Only to Delhi and a couple of places in Rajasthan.'

They talked about travelling and finished the bottle of wine. Then Nicolás said, 'I'll walk you home.' He forestalled any argument on her part by adding, 'I know I don't need to but I'd like to.'

As they walked the short distance to the *casa rural*, Cally was sharply aware that, if she turned down his job offer, they might never spend time together again.

Outside her door, he said, 'Email me when you've decided.'

'Yes, I will. Goodnight, Nicolás.' She offered her hand.

Her fingers were cold from sitting outside but his hand was warm. Warm and strong and exciting. The contact sent deep tremors through her.

'I'm not your boss yet,' he said. 'I think—in the spirit of the season—a goodnight kiss is allowable.'

At first it seemed he meant a kiss in the Spanish fashion: a brief brushing of lips against cheek, once, twice and a third time. He did kiss her cheeks, but only twice. The third kiss was on her mouth and there was nothing social about it. It was profoundly sensual, stirring her to the very depths of her being in a way that no one else's kisses ever had or ever would.

The possessive pressure of his lips filled her with an almost overwhelming longing to beg him to take her home with him and make mad, wild, delirious love to her.

He straightened and let go her hand. 'I think we've both had one glass too many,' he said.

But he looked and sounded as sober as if he'd been drinking green tea. Nor was it three glasses of wine that, for her, made the stars seem so brilliant and the night alive with promise.

'Goodnight.' He turned and strode away.

She stayed where she was till he turned the corner and vanished. Then, pulling herself together, she went inside.

Cally spent the flight to London trying to decide what to do if, at the end of her interview with Robert Quarles, he offered her a job. To turn it down would, until recently, have seemed madness. But many people would consider the job offer made by Nicolás equally, if not more, desirable.

It was not beyond possibility that even an old-established firm like Quarles would eventually succumb to the conglomeratisation of the publishing industry so that, even if she didn't lose her job a second time, her future would be governed by people whose only concern was 'the bottom line'.

Quite apart from her personal interest in him, working for Nicolás would take her into a field where exciting new developments were being made all the time and where the skills she would acquire would have many applications.

Or, she asked herself, was this line of reasoning yet more self-delusion because she could not bear to cut herself off from him?

Suddenly, as the plane was starting to land, she had a brainwave: an idea that, if she could pull it off, would give her the best of both worlds. But did she have the nerve to suggest it?

Robert Quarles received her in a beautiful, high-ceilinged room whose tall windows were curtained with pale yellow satin with tasselled tie-backs of yellow and blue cord to match the yellow and blue fringe ornamenting the pelmets. The walls were hung with oil paintings of people she took to be some of the firm's most illustrious nineteenth-century authors. It was all a far cry from the open plan modernity of most publishers' offices.

As soon as she was shown in, Mr Quarles rose from his large mahogany partners' desk and came forward to greet her. He was a tall, spare man wearing corduroy trousers and a Tattersall shirt under a tweed coat.

His manner was warm and welcoming. They had scarcely exchanged the preliminary pleasantries before a smiling girl brought in a coffee tray with blue and gold porcelain cups and a plate of interesting biscuits.

At the end of twenty minutes' discussion, Mr Quarles said, 'I think you would suit us admirably, Miss Haig. What is your feeling?'

Cally said, 'A fortnight ago I should have jumped at the chance to work for you, Mr Quarles. I've been buying and treasuring your books since I was at school. But a few days ago I was offered a job editing texts for an exciting project to do with the Internet. So I have to make a choice between two irresistible opportunities. Is there, I wonder, any possibility that I could combine the two? Could I edit for you as an out-worker, or is it essential that the successful applicant is here all the time?'

Mr Quarles looked thoughtful for some moments. Finally he said, 'We are not as dyed-in-the-wool as you might suppose. Many of our authors spend time in distant parts of the world and we keep in touch with them by email. My son is an Internet enthusiast. He has designed a website for us, which will be launched in the New Year. Yes, I think we could accommodate you, Miss Haig. But obviously not at the same salary as if you were an in-house editor.'

That evening Cally had a dinner date with Olivia and Deborah. She arrived at the house they shared some time before either of them came home. Plugging her laptop into the telephone socket in her room, she sent an email to Nicolás accepting the job with Llorca Enterprises and explaining that she was in London, tying up the loose ends of her life there. She wondered how long it would be before he replied.

Olivia came home before Deborah. She had had a wearing day. While she fixed herself a large gin and tonic, Cally explained the situation.

'But I shan't leave you in the lurch. I can pay my rent until you find a replacement for me.'

'That won't be a problem, darling,' said Olivia. 'I know of at least ten people who would give their eye teeth to live here. But are you sure you're making the right decision? Aren't you going to miss London and all the things you can do here?'

'I'll be spending time in Madrid. It has a lot to offer…wonderful art galleries and museums…palaces and parks…fabulous shops and the famous *El Rastro* flea market…'

'Yes, but there's that famous saying about the weather in Madrid. *Nueve meses de invierno, tres meses de inferno.* Nine months of winter and three months of hellish heat.'

'At least it will make a change from twelve months of mainly grey skies and rain,' said Cally, who couldn't help being mildly irritated when people spoke as if London was the centre of the world and nowhere else compared with it.

Later, with Deborah, they went for a meal at one of the many excellent restaurants in the neighbourhood. But although she always enjoyed the others' company, and loved Italian food, Cally couldn't quite suppress her impatience to check her Inbox for a reply from Nicolás.

It did not come until the following morning when she read, *Delighted by your decision. I plan to be in Valdecarrasca, but only briefly, on or about January 10th. Will drive you back to Madrid. Be prepared for very low outdoor temperatures. Nicolás.*

Predictably, Mr and Mrs Haig accepted Cally's news about her two new jobs without asking many questions. Because she wasn't sure if Nicolás wanted it kept under wraps for the time being, she did not mention his plans for La Soledad but told them as much as she knew about Llorca Enterprises.

As matters turned out it was only the eighth of January, two days after the Spanish had celebrated Three Kings, when Nicolás rang up from La Higuera to say he was back in the village but was staying only two nights and hoped she could be ready to leave at eleven o'clock the day after tomorrow. Her heart beating faster at the sound of his voice, Cally agreed that she could.

Having already said goodbye to her parents, she was ready and waiting when he came for her. Nicolás got out of the car and shook hands before picking up her suitcase and stowing it in the boot.

As they drove out of the village, he did not ask if she had enjoyed the recent festivities and she did not ask if he had.

'There's a book I'd like you to read. It's an excellent overview of the IT industry. I've put it in the pocket on your door,' he said. 'You might like to make a start on it as we're going along. You won't mind if I play a CD, I hope?'

'Not at all,' said Cally, masking her disappointment. She had been looking forward to talking to him. But merely to be in his company for however long it took to reach the capital was a secret joy.

The book, which looked rather heavy going, was actually well-written and unexpectedly absorbing. The music was a cellist, accompanied by an orchestra, playing classical pieces some of which she recognised.

Once they were on the *autopista*, the car surged forward, eating up the kilometres. They had been on the road for two hours when Nicolás stopped for petrol and suggested they had a coffee. A little before three o'clock he parked in the forecourt of a restaurant.

It was a more elegant establishment than the typical motorway cafeteria. It had tablecloths and upholstered chairs and the waiters wore uniform jackets.

When they had made their choices from an extensive menu, Nicolás leaned back in his chair and said, 'Do you find, when you're reading in your private life, that you can switch off the critical faculty you use when you're editing?'

'Not entirely. But the book you've asked me to read either didn't need much editing or has been so expertly edited that I've stayed in reader-mode. Also it's a field I don't know much about so I'm more intent on understanding it than being critical. Talking of editing, there's something I have to tell you.'

'I'm all ears.'

She explained about the letter from and interview with Robert Quarles. 'I was terribly torn. They're pretty well the last bastion of many aspects of publishing that can't survive the pressures exerted by the chain bookstores. But I also wanted to take the job with…Llorca Enterprises.' It had been on the tip of her tongue to say 'with you' but she managed a last-second switch. 'Luckily, Mr Quarles is willing to take me on as an out-worker. You have no objection to that I hope? It won't interfere with my work for your firm, I promise you.'

Nicolás saw the flicker of anxiety in her eyes. He knew enough about the British publishing world to realise that, for Cally, an offer from a house like Quarles, with a long tradition of excellence, would have been almost irresistible.

He was surprised that she hadn't grabbed it with both hands and told Llorca Enterprises to get lost, though putting it rather more politely. That she hadn't suggested that her career was not the only thing that mattered to her.

He was also reasonably sure that the job with his outfit, though it offered some interesting challenges, was not of compelling appeal to her—which encouraged him to conclude that she wasn't as resistant to the attraction between them as she made out.

He said, 'If you're sure you can cope with a dual commitment, I have no objection. But it sounds like a heavy workload. Are you certain you can handle it?'

'If I'm not living up to your expectations, I'm sure you will let me know.'

'You can rely on that,' he agreed, giving her a stern look while inwardly feeling a strong urge to reach for her hand and kiss it.

She was looking very businesslike in black trousers with a black and white check jacket over a high-necked black silk sweater. But the boardroom-style clothes couldn't disguise her essential femininity.

He had noticed in the car that she wasn't wearing the pervasive type of scent that the women in his family and many of the smartest women in Madrid favoured. But he knew, from the times he had kissed her, that her skin had a natural scent he found far more arousing than anything out of a bottle, however expensive.

It was not going to be easy keeping his word that, as long as she was his employee, he wouldn't make any further advances. But one of his few virtues was that he always kept his promises. Which meant that their personal relationship had now reached an impasse that only she could break. He wondered if she could bring herself to do it...if indeed she wanted to do it.

The only certainty was that he wanted her more than he had ever wanted anyone...more than he had ever expected to want and need a woman in his life. But that was something she was never going to find out unless she had the courage to put the past behind her and, this time, take the initiative herself.

Would she? Wouldn't she? There was no way of telling.

Meanwhile he would at least have the pleasure of looking at her and introducing her to life in Madrid.

Wondering what Nicolás was thinking as he stared out of the window beside their table, its double-glazing muffling the sound of vehicles speeding along the west-bound side of the *autopista*, Cally sensed that he wasn't best pleased by her revelation that she still had an iron in the fire in England.

'I remember at the Drydens' dinner party you said something about the Internet being the world's best hope for understanding and tolerance, but not if politicians had their way with it. Have you considered writing a book about that?' she asked.

'An excellent book has already been written by a professor at Stanford University. I'll lend it to you,' said Nicolás, surprising her with a smile instead of the severe expression that had compressed his mouth a few moments earlier.

'Actually now I come to think of it, the book you've given me to read could do with a glossary,' she said. 'For instance, the author keeps referring to fibre optics without explaining the term. Perhaps I should know what they are, but I'm afraid I don't.'

At that Nicolás gave her an even warmer smile and proceeded to explain fibre optics with a lucidity that made her feel he could have been an excellent professor himself, except that all his female students would have fallen in love with him and had difficulty keeping their minds on the subject of his lectures.

Cally's first weeks in Madrid were her happiest time since the early days at Edmund & Burke.

Its location high up among Spain's central *sierras*, at more than two thousand feet above sea level, meant that it was much colder than Valdecarrasca at about four hundred feet above the sea.

But she didn't miss the milder airs of the valley. She was both too busy and too interested in her new environment to give much thought to the weather, and anyway she would willingly have worked in Antarctica to be in occasional contact with Nicolás.

She did not see a lot of him. About once a week he stopped by her desk to ask how things were going and if she had any problems. When she said she hadn't, he chatted for a few moments and then went on his way.

Inevitably, like all bosses, he was discussed by his staff, but they all seemed solidly supportive with none of the grumbles she had often heard about her London friends' CEOs.

She had been in Madrid for a month when two surprising things happened. First she received a large envelope forwarded by the Society of Young Publishers. It contained a letter, signed 'H P Johnson (Miss)', from someone who had read *River of Life, Death and Love* and wondered if she would be interested in publishing the writer's travels during the twenty-five years since her retirement as the head of an independent school.

Cally who had read and rejected, as kindly as possible, a great many very dull memoirs by elderly people with time on their hands, felt her heart sinking. Then she read the first chapter Miss Johnson had enclosed. From the opening paragraph it was a delight, written in simple but vivid language and imbued with a delightful sense of humour. If the rest of the book lived up to this sample, it couldn't fail to sell.

The second surprise was a call from Leonora Dryden.

'Your mother gave me your telephone number. How are you liking Madrid?' she asked.

'I'm loving it,' said Cally. 'I have a tiny apartment right in the centre—it belongs to Nicolás's company and I pay a peppercorn rent—and I'm making friends and having a fabulous time.'

'I was hoping to hear that you and Nicolás might be coming back to Valdecarrasca before long. It's time I gave another party and if you two were present it would have extra pizzazz. I remember how stunning you looked at the last one.'

'I'll ask Nicolás next time I see him, but he hasn't said anything to suggest that a trip to the village might be in the offing,' said Cally.

'Have you met any of his family?' Leonora asked.

'No, but I wouldn't expect to. I'm part of his working life, not his private life, and all my new colleagues are being very friendly and hospitable. He knows I'm not lonely or at a loose end. Quite the opposite,' Cally assured her.

There was a pause before Leonora said, 'Have you been told about his mother?'

'Told what?' asked Cally, puzzled.

'His mother is a Grandee of Spain...la Duquesa de Baltasar. She lives in one of Madrid's most beautiful private palaces.'

'You're joking!' Cally said faintly. This was an even worse shock than when Luis had told her Nicolás was a billionaire.

'I assure you it's true…and his friend Simón Mondragón is another Grandee, a Marqués. I looked them both up in the *Almanach de Gotha* which lists all European nobility.'

Soon after bringing her to Madrid, Nicolás had mentioned that Cassia Mondragón had gone to stay with her mother-in-law in the country until her baby was born. Since then Cally had been too busy to give any thought to the Mondragóns.

Having no idea what a blow she had dealt, Leonora chatted for a few more minutes before saying goodbye.

It was several days—days of secret despair now that she had lost the last glimmer of hope that there was any future in loving him—before Cally saw Nicolás again.

After some conversation about the work she was doing, he astonished her by saying, 'Do you remember telling me about a Spanish autobiography, a bestseller here, which you couldn't convince Edmund & Burke's marketing people would be equally successful in translation? Would you like to meet the author?'

'Very much…but you didn't say you knew him?'

'I don't, but my mother does. She's having a *velada* tonight. I asked her if we could come. I'll pick you up at eight-thirty.'

He walked off with his usual brisk stride, leaving her wondering what, in her limited wardrobe, would be the most suitable thing to wear for a duchess's soirée.

Then, suddenly, he turned back. 'Do you have that outfit you wore at the Drydens' house with you?'

Cally nodded.

'Wear that, will you?' said Nicolás. 'I liked it.'

Damn you, she thought, as he walked away for the second

time. Why do you raise my hopes by being nice to me when you know, and I know, there isn't any future for us?

Not at all sure that his mother would approve of her outfit, Cally was ready to take the *ascensor* to ground level when, a minute before eight-thirty, her doorbell rang.

She knew that Nicolás rarely used his car in the city centre and wasn't surprised to find he had come for her in a taxi.

Sitting beside him in the back of it, she said, 'Don't you think you should have warned me your mother is a duchess? I had no idea until Mrs Dryden mentioned it during a telephone conversation the other night.'

'People of Leonora's generation tend to attach more importance to titles than I do,' he said. 'A rank inherited from someone who, centuries ago, won it by fighting—which is how most Spanish titles were achieved—is a meaningless distinction today unless it's allied to successes in other fields like those of the man you want to meet.'

'You must have a title too. Do you never use it?'

'From choice, no. Occasionally, if I have to go to a very formal function, I can't avoid it. But I duck out of those if I can. I'm only going to this *velada* because I felt you would enjoy meeting someone you admire.'

Don't do this to me, Nicolás, she thought, her heart wrung by his thoughtfulness. Aloud, she said, 'That's very kind of you. By the way, Mrs Dryden asked me if either or both of us were likely to be going to Valdecarrasca any time soon. I said I didn't think so. She's giving a party and would like to have you on her guest list.'

'I'm not planning to spend any time at La Higuera in the foreseeable future,' he said. 'If you want to go home for a long weekend you have only to say so, you know. At Llorca Enterprises, we're all grown-up, responsible people who will work flat out when it's necessary, but also take some time off when we feel the need for a break.'

'I don't,' said Cally. 'I'm enjoying Madrid too much to want to leave it even briefly.'

The taxi turned through an archway into the forecourt of a palatial building with an imposing entrance. A flight of shallow steps led up to massive doors at least twice Nicolás's height.

He gave some money to the driver and thanked him before springing out and coming round the back of the vehicle to help Cally alight. Although she was apprehensive about being presented to his mother, as they mounted the steps she was more conscious of the touch of his fingers on her elbow.

Two hours later, she found herself having a relaxed supper in a nearby restaurant with Nicolás and two of his friends who had not been at the *velada* but whom he had arranged to meet afterwards.

A married couple, both doctors, they were very different from the people she had met at the drinks party, none of whom, apart from the author of the memoir, she had warmed to.

Indeed, having met *la duquesa*, she was forced to conclude that Nicolás must take after his father who, she gathered, was no longer the duchess's husband. Not that his mother had been anything but charming to her, but it had been the artificial charm of an actress or a professional celebrity rather than a genuine warmth. Cally had been left with the feeling that the owner of the Palacio de Baltasar was, in a different way, as dissatisfied with her life as her own mother.

Knowing how difficult it had been for her, growing up with parents who did not meet each other's needs, she began to wonder if Nicolás, too, had felt alienated and that what appeared to outsiders to be privileged circumstances had, from an emotional perspective, been seriously lacking in the loving support that children and adolescents needed.

By Madrid standards, it was still early when he dropped her off at her apartment.

When she thanked him for the evening, his tone as he said, 'My pleasure,' was oddly formal.

The last time they had said goodnight, in Valdecarrasca in December, he had kissed her. Probably he had forgotten that evening. Even if he had not, clearly he was never going to kiss her again.

Walking back to his own apartment, Nicolás marvelled at his self-control. The temptation to kiss Cally goodnight had been almost irresistible, but somehow he had managed to resist it.

He wondered what she had made of the party at the *palacio* and of his mother who, according to gossip, had recently embarked on yet another of her ill-advised romances, this time with a man the same age as her elder son.

He was crossing the Plaza Santa Ana when his mobile rang. 'Nico, who was that English girl you brought to the party?' The voice was his mother's cigarette-husky drawl.

'She's an English editor I have working for me, Mama.'

'Really? I had no idea editors had so much style. One thinks of them as being serious-minded and dowdy. Are you having an affair with her?'

'No, Mama. It's a purely working relationship.' Pure being the operative word, he thought sardonically. 'Cally doesn't go in for casual affairs. Her looks are misleading. She's very serious-minded.'

'I'm sure you could change her mind if you tried,' said the *duquesa*.

'I like her mind the way it is.'

'If you aren't careful you will end up like your fa-

ther…the dullest man I have ever been married to…though
we had a lot of fun in the early days,' the *duquesa* conceded.
'Sometimes I wonder if I made a mistake in divorcing him.'

With typical casualness, she rang off without saying
goodnight, leaving Nicolás to wonder if his strategy where
Cally was concerned was not going to bring about the outcome he wanted.

As the days lengthened and Madrid lived up to its reputation
for enjoying more hours of sunshine per year than any other
European capital, Cally worked twelve-hour days converting
technical jargon into clear Spanish and English, and writing
detailed reports on the typescripts sent to her by Robert
Quarles.

In late February she flew to London for a few days, and
in March she spent a long weekend in Valdecarrasca, getting
there by train and bus. Nicolás had mentioned that the restoration of La Soledad was going ahead more slowly than
he had hoped, but the delay did not seem to concern him.
Why he had bothered to lease La Higuera when he spent
no time there was a puzzle. But presumably when one had
an income of the order that his was said to be, wasting some
of it was not the worry it would be for ordinary people.

By the middle of the month people were discussing their
plans for *Semana Santa*—the Easter holiday.

One night Cally was the last to leave the office. Thinking
herself alone in the building and hearing footsteps, she assumed it was the security guard who stayed on duty all night
and sometimes stopped by to practise his English with her.

But it was Nicolás whom she had thought was still on a
trip to the US.

'Who are you working for tonight…Quarles or Llorca
Enterprises?' he asked, pulling the chair from the neighbouring desk close to the end of her desk and sitting down.

'For Llorca Enterprises. You look rather bushed.' She had

never seen him look even mildly fatigued before and presumed it was due to jet-lag.

'It's been a hard month,' he said, 'but I'm taking some time off soon. I'm going to the Ariège…the area I told you about, on the other side of the Pyrenees. A week or ten days up there will defrag me.'

Cally watched him rake his fingers through his thick black hair in a gesture of uncharacteristic weariness. She felt something come over her: a powerful upsurge of care and concern for him.

She found herself saying, 'Would you like me to come with you?'

CHAPTER TEN

THERE was a prolonged pause during which she found it hard to hold his gaze without averting her own from his searching scrutiny.

'With what object, Cally?' he asked.

'With the object of our mutual enjoyment of a holiday like the one you suggested before and I turned down.'

'Why have you changed your mind?'

'Because I know you better now...because, as some poet said, I want to live before I die...because I think it would be fun.'

There was another disconcerting pause before he asked, 'What about Mr Right? Where does he figure in this sudden change of attitude?'

'I've decided one can't live one's life waiting for something that may never happen. The way things are is more important than future events that may not materialise.'

'I see,' said Nicolás. 'Well, I'm afraid it's too late, Cally. I've had a change of mind too, or rather a change of heart. I'm not in the market for light-hearted no-strings holiday romances any more. Perhaps I should be flattered that you've decided you're ready to have a carefree fling with me, but those days are over. You see I've fallen in love...seriously in love, with someone I want to have a permanent place in my life.'

Cally felt the bottom drop out of her world. His announcement that he had fallen in love was far more painful and shocking than anything she had felt during the period when her job with Edmund & Burke was on the line. It hurt too much for her to disguise her reaction. She stared at him horror-struck, all her pain and despair in her eyes.

He was lost to her…for ever out of reach…his heart given to someone else…someone far more suitable than she could ever be.

In a moment of excruciating insight she realised that all this time she had been deluding herself that, despite all the obstacles between them, it was still possible that one day he would come to love her.

To have that hope snatched away was the worst moment of her life.

'That's wonderful,' she said hollowly. 'I hope you'll be very happy. I—I'm sorry I've made a fool of myself.'

'On the contrary, it may be I who've made a fool of myself.'

She had no idea what he was talking about. Her brain wasn't functioning properly. It was an automatic reflex to say, 'What do you mean?'

'I don't think she knows how I feel about her.'

'Well then, tell her. What's stopping you?' she said crossly. Surely he wasn't going to add to the torture by confiding all his feelings about someone else to her.

'What if she doesn't feel the same way?' said Nicolás.

'She will feel the same…I'm sure she will.'

She marvelled at her own self-control. How could she be discussing this like a relationship counsellor when she wanted to run away and hide in some dark private corner where no one would witness the depths of her wretchedness?

'I think we have our wires crossed, Cally. It's you I'm talking about. You've offered to go to the mountains with me, but how do you feel about marrying me?'

'What?' she said blankly.

A smile flickering round his mouth, he said, 'I will take you to the Ariège with the greatest pleasure, but on one condition: that you promise to marry me as soon as possible after we get back.'

Then, closing the gap between them and placing his hands on her shoulders, he said in a more serious tone, 'I love you. I've been patiently waiting for a sign that it might be mutual. Is it?'

It took a few moments for it to sink in that he wasn't fooling. He meant it. Nicolás, the unattainable, felt the same way about her as she did about him.

She took a deep shaky breath. 'Of course it is, idiot!' she said, half laughing, half crying.

And then Nicolás pulled her against him and kissed her in a way he never had before, with what she recognised as the same blissful relief that she was feeling.

Some time later, he said, 'Let's find a quiet restaurant where we can talk…or, a better idea, let's go back to my place and have a meal brought to us there. How does that sound to you?'

It was clear to Cally that if she agreed to this plan she would be spending the night with him. 'It sounds wonderful,' she said happily.

The security officer was in the lobby as they left the building.

'You can be the first to congratulate me, Vicente,' said Nicolás. 'Señorita Haig has just agreed to marry me.'

'That's wonderful news, sir,' said Vicente, shaking hands with him. 'My wife will be thrilled when I tell her.' He turned to Cally. 'My wife was badly injured in an accident two years ago. If it hadn't been for Don Nicolás helping us, she wouldn't have made such a good recovery…and we're not the only people he's helped. You'll never hear about it from him, but your *novio* is one of the kindest people I've ever known. I don't mean to sound impertinent, but you're a lucky young lady to be marrying him.'

'Vicente exaggerates,' said Nicolás.

It was the first time Cally had seen him look embarrassed. Ignoring his comment, she said to the security guard, 'I know I am, but I'm going to do my best to be the wife he deserves.'

'I shall hold you to that,' said Nicolás, putting an arm round her. His tone was teasing but there was tenderness as well as amusement in his eyes.

They walked through the city centre arm in arm, their fingers entwined. Madrid, always smarter and livelier than London at night, had never seemed more glamorous.

The entrance to the block of apartments where Nicolás lived was in a fashionable pedestrians-only street lined with some of the city's most exclusive clothes shops and jewellers. His apartment was on the top floor. As he showed her into the large living room, Cally saw that one wall was lined with books, another with paintings and a third wall consisted of huge plate glass floor-to-ceiling windows with, beyond them, a discreetly illuminated roof garden.

'Let me take your coat,' said Nicolás.

While she unfastened the buttons of her classic wool coat, an investment made with her first Llorca Enterprises pay. cheque, he positioned himself behind her to help her slide her arms from the sleeves.

Even when the weather had been at its coldest, she had never seen him wear an overcoat. His only concession to the cold had been a navy blue cashmere scarf wound twice round his neck. She had concluded that his running kept his circulation at a level that made him impervious to temperatures that made other men huddle inside their expensive loden coats.

He laid her coat over the back of a chair. 'Are you starving?'

'Not for food.'

'That's what I hoped you would say.'

He began to press soft kisses on her forehead, her eyebrows and her eyelids, working his way slowly towards her eager lips.

Presently, as their mouths met and fused, his hands began to explore the contours of her body with light but thrillingly intimate caresses that made her tremble with impatience to feel his fingers and palms on her naked skin.

For so many lonely nights she had tossed and turned, tormented by images conjured up by her imagination that had seemed to have no hope of ever being fulfilled. Now that, at last, she was here in his arms, suddenly all her inhibitions evaporated. She began to unbutton her shirt, her fingers made clumsy by haste to be rid of it.

Nicolás broke off the kiss and stopped stroking her, but only in order to unfasten his own shirt. As, not for the first time, she saw the broad shoulders exposed and the hard male chest laid bare, Cally drew in a ragged breath. He had looked magnificent in his running kit, but stripped to the waist he looked even better.

He seemed equally eager to see her top half exposed and, after tugging his shirt free from his trousers and shrugging it off, he reached for the hem of her white silk camisole and drew it higher and higher until it cleared her raised arms and he could toss it aside and reach round behind her to unclip her lacy bra.

As that, too, was tossed aside, he said, 'I've been dreaming of this moment since that day we went to La Soledad and you were frightened by a snake. Do you remember? I do. For one unforgettable moment, I felt your breast fit my palm.' His dark eyes burned with ardour she had never seen before. Speaking in Spanish, his voice low and husky, he said, 'Now they are mine to caress whenever I want. But what I want now is to feel them against me.' He put his hands on her waist and drew her closer and closer until the softness of her flesh was pressed to the muscular hardness of his.

Cally slid her arms upwards until her elbows were resting on his shoulders and she could enjoy caressing the back of his neck.

'This feels wonderful,' she murmured.

'Mmm…I agree…but let's go somewhere more private.'

With easy strength he picked her up and carried her through a doorway into another room where, in the light from the living room, she could see a wide bed.

Nicolás set her down on one side of it and tapped a couple of buttons on a control box on the night table. One activated reading lamps on either side of the bed. The other controlled long curtains which swished softly across another expanse of glass overlooking the terrace.

'Is that your bathroom?' she asked, looking at an inner door.

'Yes…do you want to use it? Go ahead.'

When, three or four minutes later, she emerged from the bathroom, having shed her skirt, tights and panties, she found Nicolás, too, had finished stripping off. He had also removed the bedcover and the top layer of bedclothes.

'I used your toothbrush. I hope that's all right?'

He gave her his bone-melting smile. 'Isn't sharing a toothbrush one of the key tests of love? I need to brush my teeth too. Be right back.'

Cally lay down to wait for him, feeling as if all her life the world had been like a picture hanging slightly askew which now was hanging straight.

He came back and stretched his long frame beside hers, propping himself on one elbow in order to look into her eyes. 'There were times when I thought we should never reach this point,' he said quietly. 'The months since I've known you have seemed like years.'

She smiled at him. 'But now we're here and I'm all

yours…longing for you to make love to me.' As she had once before, a long time ago, she put her hands up to touch the high cheekbones, the forceful jaw. 'I feel as if I have loved you all my life…that, in my heart, I recognised you the day you came to the door in Valdecarrasca.'

'And I you,' he told her softly.

Then the longing repressed by them both for so long became overwhelming and, as Nicolás's lips and hands began to caress her in new ways, Cally found that somehow she had lost all her inhibitions and knew instinctively how to respond to him.

She surfaced from a deep sleep, thinking it must be morning. Then, looking at her watch, which she had been too excited take off earlier, she saw it was only an hour and a half since she had been at her desk, never dreaming that tomorrow and all the days after it would be part of the new life begun so rapturously this evening.

She was wondering if she could reach across Nicolás to switch out the lights without disturbing him, when he stirred and gave a deep sigh of what she hoped was unconscious contentment. For herself, in both mind and body, she had never felt more relaxed.

Suddenly, when she thought he was going to sink into an even deeper sleep, he woke, his dark eyes snapping open, fully alert and bright with renewed vitality.

'How long have you been awake?' he asked, smiling.

Cally smiled back. 'Only a minute or two.'

Nicolás turned towards her and pushed himself up on one elbow, his other hand stroking her hair away from her temples. 'Are you exhausted? Is it too soon to make love again?'

'I don't feel as if I'm exhausted. You're the one who claimed to be frazzled. I would never have guessed it,' she teased him.

Nicolás gave the soft laugh that sent tingles down her spine. 'You have a revitalising effect on me.'

It was even better the second time. With each kiss, each caress Cally felt their understanding of each other deepening. Why had he ever seemed an enigma when now he seemed the one person who, as time went on, she would come to know almost as intimately as she knew herself?

Afterwards, as they lay locked together, the rapid pounding of their hearts gradually subsiding to a normal beat, she slid her hands down his long back and touched her lips to his shoulder, inhaling the smell of his skin. Unlike most Spanish men, he did not use strong cologne. She liked his natural scent better.

Presently, Nicolás eased himself gently away. 'I'm going to open a bottle and then we'll decide what to eat.'

He sprang off the bed and went to the bathroom, reappearing moments later with a towel wrapped round his hips and over his arm a dark silk dressing gown she had vaguely noticed hanging behind the door.

'This will drown you but it's the best I can offer,' he said, holding it ready for her to put on.

Cally scrambled off the bed and plunged her arms into the sleeves, thinking how different her body felt now compared with when he had helped her take off her coat. Then, although not a virgin, she had never known what it was to feel wholly possessed and fulfilled. Now she did.

Nicolás wrapped the robe round her while kissing the back of her neck, his hands smoothing the silk into place in a way that was meant to amuse her, and did, but also started another buzz of excitement. She knew that if he had wanted to take her a third time she would have consented eagerly.

In his kitchen, Nicolás produced a folder containing details of the food on offer at every takeout place in the centre of the city. While he opened a bottle of wine, Cally looked through them.

'Do you live on takeout food?'

'Mostly I eat out. Why cook when there are twenty professionals doing it a short walk away? I've only used the takeouts occasionally. They're not as good as in New York, but they're not bad.'

When their supper had been chosen and ordered, he said, 'Do you want to call your parents tonight, or shall we drive down tomorrow and tell them in person?'

'I thought we were going to the Ariège? Can't I ring them from there? You aren't going to have to introduce me to all your relations, are you?' asked Cally, daunted by the thought of a long round of family presentations when all she wanted was to be alone with him.

'No, that isn't necessary. But I think I should pay a courtesy visit to your parents. My mother you can meet again when we get back from our trip. It's not much of a detour to Valdecarrasca.'

Next day, as they drove back the way they had come in January, Cally spent a lot of time gazing, with wonder and delight, at the antique emerald ring that Nicolás had fetched from his bank earlier that morning. She had always thought emeralds the most beautiful of all the precious stones and when Nicolás had offered the ring as a placeholder until there was time to select a permanent engagement ring, she had asked if she could keep this one.

He had said, 'Of course…if you're sure you like it. It belonged to my paternal grandmother who left all her jewels to me for my future wife.'

During their lunch stop Nicolás said, 'I'm having second thoughts about La Soledad. Perhaps I should relocate the website design centre and keep the house for our personal use. It was a family house once…it could be again.'

'Isn't it much too large for a modern family house?' Cally said doubtfully.

'I wasn't thinking only of you and me and however many children we decide to have. When he retires, my father might like to have a place in the country where he can be with us but not on top of us. In a few years' time your parents may want to sell the *casa rural* and take life more easily. In Spain, the elderly aren't packed off to live in ''homes'' with other old people as often as they are in other countries.'

'I know,' said Cally, thinking of ancient Señora Martinez, still living with her descendants, probably driving them mad sometimes, but not ending her days in an unfamiliar environment with only occasional visits from her relations. 'But do you really want to take on my parents as well as me?'

'I'm not suggesting we should live at La Soledad all the time...only sometimes...whenever it suits us.'

The Haigs' reaction to the news that their daughter was engaged to a Spaniard was, as Cally had expected, somewhat guarded. But as yet they were not aware that their future son-in-law was no ordinary Madrileño. For a couple who had lived abroad so long they were still oddly insular in outlook.

Juanita and the Drydens, on whom she and Nicolás called later, were more enthusiastic.

'I knew you were made for each other,' said Juanita, embracing them both.

A little later, Leonora said, 'I'm beginning to think that La Higuera has a romantic influence on people who spend time under its roof. How long are you staying?'

'Only tonight,' said Nicolás. 'Tomorrow we're heading north for an unofficial honeymoon before we tackle the matter of where and how to get married. We both have a lot of friends who will expect an invitation and I also have a horde of relations who will be offended if they don't get one.'

*   *   *

Even in Nicolás's car it would have been a twelve-hour run from Valdecarrasca to their destination on the French side of the Pyrenees.

'I don't want you arriving too exhausted to make love,' he said, teasingly. 'We'll spend the first night at the *parador* in the castle at Cardona.'

During the drive to Cardona he told her a bit of the castle's history.

'It has a tower called the Torre Minyona. In Catalan, *minyona* means a maid...a young girl...a virgin. In the eleventh century, Adalés, the daughter of the castle's owner, fell in love with the Moor who was warden of the castle of Malda. Even though the Moor renounced Islam for her, the religious problem was considered so great that her parents and brothers condemned her to live in the tower with only a dumb servant to keep her company. Not surprisingly, she became ill and died a year later.'

It was easy for Cally to identify with the desperate girl, shut away with no hope of seeing the man she loved.

'What appalling cruelty. Couldn't he have rescued her...carried her off?'

'I expect he thought about it, but when you see the castle, you'll understand how impossible it would have been.'

The sun shone all the way and they shared the driving, Nicolás having greater confidence in her skills than she had. He actually cat-napped while she was at the wheel. It seemed that, in addition to all his other qualities, he was one of those rare men who did not feel themselves automatically superior to every woman driver on the road. After some initial nervousness, Cally began to get used to the car and its controls, and to enjoy driving it.

They stopped for coffee breaks and took an hour for a light lunch, but drank only mineral water, reserving wine for the evening.

As she thought of the night ahead, her third night sharing his bed, her heart beat an excited tattoo.

It was late afternoon when they saw the great mediaeval fortress soaring against the sky on the crest of a hill. It looked impregnable.

But their suite in the Castle's *parador* was luxuriously comfortable and a bottle of the best *cava*—the Spanish equivalent of champagne—was waiting for them in an ice bucket.

'Some champagne…a shower…and then a rest before dinner. How does that sound?' said Nicolás, when the porter who had brought up their baggage had been tipped and gone on his way.

'Sounds perfect. Do they always greet guests with *cava* in *paradores*?' She had never stayed in one before.

Nicolás smiled. 'I emailed our expected time of arrival and asked them to have it ready. But first…a kiss.' He reached out a long arm and drew her to him. 'It's a shame that Adalés and her Moor never enjoyed this moment.'

Cally put her arms round his waist and rested her forehead against his chest. 'I can't bear to think of them being so unhappy. I've been pretty miserable myself, but at least I was seeing you…working for you…not shut away like a criminal. The worst of it is that those sort of stupid prejudices are still keeping people apart, hundreds of years later.'

'Stupidity isn't likely to die out any time soon, but I don't think we need to worry about it right now.' His fingers under her chin, he tilted her face up to his. 'You are so beautiful. I was watching you while you were driving. You were intent on the road. I could watch you for hours and never grow bored as one does with the pretty, empty faces in magazines and on TV.'

Cally had flown over the Pyrenees many times but never travelled by road over that formidable barrier between the eastern half of France and the northern provinces of Spain.

'During World War Two, there was an escape route—
le chemin de la liberté—from Nazi-occupied France through
these mountains,' said Nicolás. 'Refugees, resistance fight-
ers, Allied pilots who had had to bale out, they all toiled up
through the passes from the other side with inadequate
clothing and provisions. Now there's a great subject that
your author Rhys might like to tackle…if it hasn't been
done already.'

'I'll check it out,' said Cally, thinking how wonderful it
would be always to have someone as well-read as Nicolás
as a sounding-board for her professional thoughts and problems.

When she mentioned this during dinner, he said, 'That's
why I held off from marriage…because I could see that it
had to be a partnership on a lot of levels, and until I met
you I never had that kind of total rapport with anyone. Body,
mind and soul is a complex match that I don't think happens
too often, but seems to have happened with us.'

'Which is strange, considering how different our backgrounds are.'

'Different superficially perhaps, but not when you get
down to basics. Until now we've both been loners…not
anti-social loners, but loners in the sense of having to rely
on ourselves from an early age in a way that the children
of happy families don't.'

Later, as they went upstairs together, Cally was struck by
how quickly it had come to seem natural to be spending the
night with him.

It was hard, now, to believe that only a few days ago he
had seemed as remote and inaccessible as the summits of
the mountains they had crossed. Yet in a very short time
they would have shed their clothes and be locked in a pas-

sionate embrace. And all it had taken to achieve that amazing change was the courage to risk a rebuff.

As soon as he had unlocked the door of their room, and closed it again behind them, Nicolás took her in his arms as impatiently as if it had been several days, not less than a couple of hours, since their last kiss.

Cally relaxed against him and closed her eyes, waiting for the delicious moment when their mouths would meet.

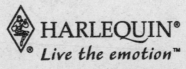

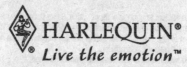

If you enjoyed what you just read,
then we've got an offer you can't resist!

Take 2 bestselling love stories FREE!

Plus get a FREE surprise gift!

Clip this page and mail it to Harlequin Reader Service®

IN U.S.A.
3010 Walden Ave.
P.O. Box 1867
Buffalo, N.Y. 14240-1867

IN CANADA
P.O. Box 609
Fort Erie, Ontario
L2A 5X3

YES! Please send me 2 free Harlequin Romance® novels and my free surprise gift. After receiving them, if I don't wish to receive anymore, I can return the shipping statement marked cancel. If I don't cancel, I will receive 6 brand-new novels every month, before they're available in stores! In the U.S.A., bill me at the bargain price of $3.34 plus 25¢ shipping & handling per book and applicable sales tax, if any*. In Canada, bill me at the bargain price of $3.80 plus 25¢ shipping & handling per book and applicable taxes**. That's the complete price and a savings of 10% off the cover prices—what a great deal! I understand that accepting the 2 free books and gift places me under no obligation ever to buy any books. I can always return a shipment and cancel at any time. Even if I never buy another book from Harlequin, the 2 free books and gift are mine to keep forever.

186 HDN DNTX
386 HDN DNTY

Name	(PLEASE PRINT)	
Address	Apt.#	
City	State/Prov.	Zip/Postal Code

* Terms and prices subject to change without notice. Sales tax applicable in N.Y.
** Canadian residents will be charged applicable provincial taxes and GST.
   All orders subject to approval. Offer limited to one per household and not valid to
   current Harlequin Romance® subscribers.
   ® are registered trademarks of Harlequin Enterprises Limited.

HROM02   ©2001 Harlequin Enterprises Limited

In *Changing Habits,* *New York Times* bestselling author Debbie Macomber proves once again why she's one of the world's most popular writers of fiction for—and about—women.

DEBBIE MACOMBER

They were sisters once.

In a more innocent time, three girls enter the convent. Angelina, Kathleen and Joanna come from very different backgrounds, but they have one thing in common— the desire to join a religious order.

Despite the seclusion of the convent house in Minneapolis, they're not immune to what's happening around them, and each sister faces an unexpected crisis of faith. Ultimately Angie, Kathleen and Joanna all leave the sisterhood, abandoning the convent for the exciting and confusing world outside. The world of choices to be made, of risks to be taken. Of men and romantic love. The world of ordinary women...

CHANGING HABITS

"Macomber offers a very human look at three women who uproot their lives to follow their true destiny."
—*Booklist*

Available the first week of April 2004 wherever paperbacks are sold.

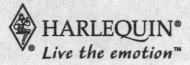

Do you like stories that get *up close* and *personal*?
Do you long to be loved *truly, madly, deeply…*?

If you're looking for emotionally intense, tantalizingly
tender love stories, stop searching and start reading

Harlequin Romance®

You'll find authors who'll leave you breathless, including:

Liz Fielding
Winner of the 2001 RITA Award for
Best Traditional Romance
(The Best Man and the Bridesmaid)

Day Leclaire
USA Today bestselling author

Leigh Michaels
Bestselling author with 30 million
copies of her books sold worldwide

Renee Roszel
USA Today bestselling author

Margaret Way
Australian star with 80 novels to her credit

Sophie Weston
A fresh British voice and a hot talent!

Don't miss their latest novels, coming soon!

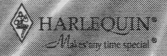

HARLEQUIN®
Makes any time special®